DEVOTED TO AN *Outlaw* 2

A NOVEL BY
DAK

© 2019 Royalty Publishing House

Published by Royalty Publishing House
www.royaltypublishinghouse.com

ALL RIGHTS RESERVED
Any unauthorized reprint or use of the material is prohibited. No part of this book may be reproduced or transmitted in any form or by any means, electronic or mechanical, including photocopying, recording, or by any information storage without express permission by the author or publisher. This is an original work of fiction. Names, characters, places and incidents are either products of the author's imagination or are used fictitiously and any resemblance to actual persons, living or dead, is entirely coincidental.
Contains explicit language & adult themes suitable for ages 16+ only.

Royalty Publishing House is now accepting manuscripts from aspiring or experienced urban romance authors!

WHAT MAY PLACE YOU ABOVE THE REST:

Heroes who are the ultimate book bae: strong-willed, maybe a little rough around the edges but willing to risk it all for the woman he loves.

Heroines who are the ultimate match: the girl next door type, not perfect - has her faults but is still a decent person. One who is willing to risk it all for the man she loves.

The rest is up to you! Just be creative, think out of the box, keep it sexy and intriguing!

If you'd like to join the Royal family, send us the first 15K words (60 pages) of your completed manuscript to submissions@royaltypublishinghouse.com

SYNOPSIS

After dealing with a tragic loss, Havoc is trying to figure out how to balance his life raising a kid while revenge is on his mind. With Biz still walking around, Havoc is bound to do just about anything to make sure his days are limited. He's willing to get just about anyone on his side who hates Biz as much as he does..

Meanwhile, Ivory is trying to find his way. Retracing the steps of his past, the only thing on his mind is avenging his parents' death. Unsure of where to go to put the pieces together, he goes back to where it all went bad for him, reliving the memories of his past. When the truth comes out, Ivory is torn on how to handle it and unsure if he can.

Bonnie and Biz are trying to get this thing called love right, but when things take a turn for the worst it seems that Biz may have his hands fuller than he can handle. While trying to be a dad, Biz is also trying to be a friend to Missy. But as she becomes a distraction, Bonnie's radar is alert.

CHAPTER 1

"I'm an outlaw, got an outlaw chick."

— JAY-Z

"*D*rive somewhere in the open, with a lot of traffic and pedestrians," Bonnie instructed Biz as she sat back in her seat and put her head against the headrest. Her emotions were at an all-time high, but being the gangster bitch she was, she managed to keep them in check. She couldn't believe that Khalil had betrayed her the way he did, and she didn't feel an ounce of guilt for killing Harper. She knew that Harper was telling the truth about the situation, because what other reason would she have wanted Khalil dead? She hadn't seen it before but the resemblance between Khalil and CJ was uncanny, and she couldn't deny it. All these years, and she began to think was any of it true. The love he had claimed he had for her seemed to vanish in the blink of an eye. A real nigga would've come clean about it and let her make the decision of staying or leaving, and a real friend would've done the same. But it was apparent that they were both frauds with their own agendas. The little bit of guilt she had once felt for falling in love with Biz was now nonexistent. She had been played first and a small part of her was happy that it had happened in that way. Now she could move forward with her life without questioning if she was wrong for falling in love with who was supposed to be her enemy. All along she had been sleeping with the enemy. And the thought alone made her sick to her stomach. She had thought Khalil was for her, but it was clear it was all a façade. A nigga did what he had to do to get a bitch but then once he got her, he didn't know what to do with her or how to keep her. She took a deep breath at the thought, dwelling on the situation as minimally as she dwelled on death, right before pushing it to the back of her mind.

Biz pulled into a parking lot of Six Flags and as soon as the car came to a halt, she jumped out and got into the backseat. Biz didn't say a word. Bonnie had passed his test and proven her loyalty to him, and she had regained his trust. He watched from the rearview mirror as she began dumping the money out the bag. She knew her twin brother just as well as she knew herself. After emptying the bag, she pulled out a pocket knife that was kept under the seat and began to make small slits in the bag until she found what she was looking for. After about five minutes, she found it; a micro mini tracker. She shook her head before passing it to Biz. She dumped the money out the second duffle bag and passed it to Biz and watched as he stepped out the car and dropped the duffle bag off next to another car and kicking it underneath.

Bonnie knew there was no way that Havoc was going to just take an L of a hundred million dollars. That pretty penny was putting a dent in his pockets and she knew it. As she thought of her brother and how he was with Harper, she began to get angry with him as well. She felt like there was no way that he couldn't have known. He and Khalil were boys and told each other everything. He had actually shown Bonnie that he would go to war with her for Khalil so she felt in her heart that the whole time, the three of them were in on this big secret that she knew nothing about. She shook her head as Biz got back into the car and there they were driving off into the sunset, as if Bonnie hadn't just ended someone's life. A hundred million dollars richer, Biz was ready to take over his company again with his lady on his arm. Havoc had crippled him causing him to start back at square one but with Bonnie by his side, he knew it wasn't impossible. She had been his best hitta from the very beginning and with her by his side, they would flourish.

As Bonnie put her head back on the headrest and placed her hand over her belly, Biz looked over at his woman and flashed her one of his rare and infamous smiles. "You down for a nigga?" he questioned, knowing the answer instantly but still wanting to hear the actual words come out of her mouth. Bonnie leaned over the armrest placing her lips on his. He had no idea the clouds he put her on. Just a simple kiss made her soul leave the earth and sit at the gates of heaven. She pulled back and grabbed her shades from the center console and slid them on her face.

"Till the wheels fall off," she said while turning back in her seat facing the road. Biz placed his hand on her thigh giving it a light squeeze. A squeeze that was enough to make Bonnie want to take him down right there in the car. It had been long overdue and she was in desperate need of his pipe game. She wasn't going to say a word though. Words couldn't put together how much she needed him to fill her up. But actions? Baby, actions spoke louder than any words that she could possibly speak. She allowed him to caress her leg, letting that be all the foreplay that she needed. To her, living in a house with Biz and being unable to touch him was enough foreplay. She had enough foreplay to last her a lifetime and wasn't going to waste another minute on it.

As the car came to a halt in front of their house, Biz cut off the engine and hopped out as Bonnie remained seated. Without uttering a word to him, he knew exactly what it was she was waiting on. He shook his head while walking over to her door and holding his hand out for her to latch onto before getting out. She flashed him a smile while giggling. Any man that wanted to deal with her had to deal with her accordingly. She was a lady and was to be treated as such at all times. It didn't matter how gangster or tough a man was. To his lady, he had to be a gentleman first. That was exactly Bonnie's type. A 'gangster gentleman.'

"Spoiled ass," Biz commented as they walked to the front door. Bonnie just raised her brows and rubbed his arm.

"Oh you ain't seen spoiled yet playa," she responded while walking into the house. The first thing she did was kick off her shoes and then she was down to business.

Without another word, she was stripping out of her garments and Biz already knew what time it was. "Fuck me, right here, right now!" she demanded. She had no clue that, that was all she needed to say. Standing before him in her birthday suit, he wanted to do nothing more than what she had just asked for. He rushed over to her, scooping her off the ground as if she weighed the same amount as a feather. With their mouths glued to one another, they both spoke in a foreign language that only the two of them could understand. The thought of carrying her up the stairs crossed his mind but instantly he went against it. He wanted to feel her insides right this minute and going up the stairs would only prolong it.

He laid her on the couch and went straight to her feet. He brushed his tongue across each of her toes and a small moan escaped her lips. Her moaning so softly made him want to plunge into her, but patience was the key. He wanted to make every part of her feel good before he got his. His hands roamed freely around her body feeling the softness of her skin. His hands went from her breasts to her love box and the juices that seeped out of her were calling for him. He positioned her body on the chair so that she could stay comfortable, and got on his knees sticking his lips directly on her pair of southern lips. "Ahh," she moaned, and he continued to take his time as he stuck his tongue in and out of her, making sure to savor every single taste. With his hands on her ass, squeezing while helping to move her closer to him, he devoured her like a meal out of a five-star restaurant.

He had no idea that he was driving her crazy. She wanted to run from him but with it feeling so good, she wanted to just stay and let him do his thing. She tried using her mind to control herself, but it was of no use as her body began to shudder and that familiar feeling came over her. She squeezed the couch cushion and just when she couldn't hold it in anymore, she exploded right in his mouth. It was exactly what he wanted. What he had anticipated. To him, her juices were juices of gold and he hadn't tasted anything like it. He licked her clean and stood to his feet.

Bonnie was two steps ahead of him. She began to pull on the waistband of his sweats and the minute his dick was out Bonnie's mouth was glued to it. The same way Biz thought there was no better taste in the world except Bonnie, she felt like he was the richest taste in the world. The way that the two of them admired every part of one another, it was another reason why their connection was so strong. Bonnie's head bobbed up and down as Biz stood tall running his hand through her hair. As the veins began to protrude from his manhood, Bonnie began to speed up her process. Just as he was about to nut he pulled back from her, standing her up. He picked her up and she wrapped her legs around his waist as he slid into her pumping in and out of her.

"AHHHHH!! OH MY GOD!" she yelled as he pumped in and out of her with a force so strong that she had no other choice but to cum. But that didn't stop him. He continued to flex in and out of her and just as she was about to cum her third time, this time they both came at the same time. Bonnie placed her head on his chest, and with his dick still inside her he took a seat on the couch.

This was what they'd both wanted for so long and at first it seemed like it was almost impossible but here they were, doing the impossible. As their heartbeats began to slow down, Bonnie put her head into the crook of his neck. This moment right here, right now was what Biz had in his mind as perfect. He had met his soulmate, and there was no denying it. He had denied her for so long that he didn't want to think of that anymore.

"It's only up from here B, a nigga got you," he promised while wrapping his toned arms around her body and giving her a light squeeze.

The sound of that was music to Bonnie's ears. She loved Biz more than she knew and to know that he loved her the same was all the assurance she needed.

"I love you nigga," she said while giving him a kiss on his neck.

He nodded his head before replying, "I know, a nigga love the shit out you too B."

CHAPTER 2

BLOOD ON MY HANDS

"It's something I'm not revealing. Though you got used to my disguise, you can't shake this awful feeling."

— THE USED

The confirmation of Harper's entrance into the gates of heaven put Havoc somewhat at ease, as he sat in his car letting the rain soothe a crying CJ to sleep. Havoc knew that there were many things in life that CJ would get past, but this wasn't one of them. He had watched his mother get murdered in cold blood, witnessed her last breaths and he was sure the young boy had a million questions on his mind. CJ wasn't the only one though. Havoc had been so blindsided by everything that was going on that when the truth revealed itself, it was like a combo of slaps and punches. So many of his questions had remained unanswered and he had no idea how to handle that. For someone who got answers when he demanded them, right now he was thrown for a loop and wasn't his regular self. Before leaving the exchange point, he shot the maids a text. And just like that, he knew Harper's corpse would be handled.

He drove off the premises heading towards his house with his mind heavier than he had intended it being. One minute he was planning his future with Harper and the next he was drenched in her blood by the hands of his twin sister. He knew that Bonnie killing her was justifiable and that was why he didn't hold an inch of anger towards her about the death. The anger that radiated from him was because he felt like Biz deserved to die as well for being the one to actually pull the trigger on Khalil. His mind began to ponder on whether Biz and Bonnie had planned this all along. It was just so crazy how everything seemed to fall in their favor. Bonnie was pregnant with Biz's baby and that alone let him know for sure that he had gotten played by his sister. He wasn't 100% sure on how things unfolded and didn't care to find out. His beef with Biz was now bigger than Khalil's death. It now also had to do with the fact that his twin sister had picked Biz over her flesh and blood.

He pulled up to his house and looked at his rearview mirror, setting his sights on a sleeping CJ. The tear stains on his face didn't go unnoticed. Havoc hated that he had gone through what he went through, but what was done was done. CJ had been a fatherless child all along but now here he was motherless as well. Havoc knew nothing about what to do with CJ. At least his way of raising a child wasn't what CJ was used to, and he was almost sure that it wasn't the way that Harper nor Khalil would've wanted him raised. But what was he really supposed to do? Give him up to the system? That wasn't even a factor in his mind because he himself had gone through the system for a while and it wasn't the best experience. He was conflicted when he felt like he shouldn't have been. But he knew that his confliction came from the bond that he and Harper had, as well as the bond that he and Khalil had.

He got out the car and opened the rear door carrying CJ to the house as the rain began to drench their clothes. Before he could even open the door, Ivory swung it open and before he could say a word, the first thing he noticed was the blood on their clothing. A worried look was on his face as he looked behind Havoc looking for Harper and without a word, when their eyes connected, Ivory knew that she was gone. His heart instantly saddened, and he didn't know what to say or do and decided not to do anything. He stepped aside letting Havoc in and watched as he went into the bedroom. He had questions of his own but he knew that now wasn't the time. He had obviously missed out on a lot and with the look on Havoc's face, he needed time to himself to recuperate. Ivory took a seat on the couch feeling like Havoc had made the wrong call when it came to him staying home. He had been obedient and listened and everything went left. He sat sulking in his thoughts, not daring to bring any of them up to Havoc.

Almost an hour later, Havoc exited his bedroom and entered the living room accompanying Ivory on the couch. They both knew one another well enough to know that something was on their minds and neither of them wanted to break the ice. Ivory wasn't sure where to start with his questioning and just decided to let Havoc reveal what he wanted. "B is alive, and so is Biz."

Ivory didn't say a word, but his face said enough. Putting two and two together, he spoke up, "And they are together? They had CJ?"

Havoc nodded his head.

"And Harper?" he questioned. He knew she was dead but why had she been a casualty was more so his question.

"B killed her. CJ is Khalil's son. Man, this shit is crazy, and saying it makes a nigga feel crazier. So much shit been going on and a nigga been in the dark. But like they say, everything that happens in the dark comes to light and today, the motherfucking light was shining brighter than a motherfucker."

"Damn, you need me to handle them?" Ivory asked.

Havoc shook his head. He knew that he wouldn't get close enough to Bonnie or Biz to shake their hand let alone kill them. He knew that sending Ivory out to hunt them down was a suicide mission and right now, for the first time in his life, he didn't want any death happening around him. He had taken away so many lives that death had become second nature to him. He had kept his circle tight, so death never crept up on them. But with the death of Khalil and Harper, right now he was feeling it. He knew how the pain felt that he had put so many families through and though it had all been business, these deaths to him had been personal. He knew he had to catch Biz on his own time. But right now, shit was hot, and he needed for it to cool down before he made a move.

"Well do you at least want me to get the bread back?" Ivory pressed. And again, he shook his head from side to side.

"The bread long gone," he confirmed, knowing that Bonnie knew about the tracking device. It had been a thing that the two of them did. Had he known that she was down on this plan, he would have gone about things completely different.

"So, what's the plan?" Ivory asked.

Havoc stood from his seat and looked down on Ivory. "There ain't no plan yet Ivory. There's sheets in the closet, a nigga gon' lay down and get his shit together and tomorrow, a new day, we'll talk business," he said before walking away and into his room.

CJ was still in the bed sleeping, and Havoc just shook his head. He knew that if he kept CJ he would turn out just like himself and Ivory, and he wasn't sure if that was a good or bad thing. At six years old, he had seen shit he had no business seeing and Havoc knew that it would change him. CJ had witnessed first-hand how cruel people in the world could be. Even people that he trusted were capable of betraying him. CJ had been betrayed by Bonnie, but Havoc felt like he had been betrayed by everyone that he was willing to put his life on the line for. He wanted to just let it all go and move forward with his life, but he knew there was no way. Biz was alive and he knew that there would be a fight for the company, and Havoc wasn't willing to fall back. Especially not after taking a loss of a hundred mil. Although Bonnie had killed Harper for Khalil, Havoc still wanted Biz dead. He had killed

Khalil and corrupted his sister and also impregnated her. To him, Biz had gotten away with too much for him to just walk away.

He laid on the bed looking up at the ceiling, trying to piece together a plan. But with so much on his mind, he knew that no plan that he could come up with would be a good one. He needed a clear mind before planning anything.

"I love you Mommy," CJ said in his sleep causing Havoc to look over at him. As he looked at CJ, he saw himself. It was as if he had gone back in time and CJ was the youngest version of him and Ivory was the junior. The pain that CJ was going through, Havoc knew of too well. He also knew that there was no greater pain in the world than losing a mother, and that alone would make CJ invincible. Losing a dad was always a blow to the face. But losing a mother, who was a damn good mother, was the worst feeling any kid could feel.

Havoc closed his eyes wanting sleep to take over, but every time, all he could see was a dying Harper. He couldn't understand why her death had hit him so hard, but in reality, it was because he had let her in more than he had intended. He had already engraved it in his mind and heart that he would be her protector and failed miserably at it. No other death had hit this hard for him, and actually revealing to himself the truth that she had his heart was too much. He couldn't, he wasn't supposed to fall for any woman. But he had, and now he was regretting it. The truth of his feelings for her were all showing, and he had no control over it. He needed something to take his mind off of her and knew just the trick. He hadn't smoked in years but right now it was more of a need than want. He stood from the bed and went into the living room.

"Ivory, you got that purple pack on you?" he asked. And Ivory sat up giving him a smirk. Havoc had always told him not to smoke but that was the one habit that he couldn't push. Weed made him feel good and he was good on limiting himself on how much he smoked. He felt like as long as he smoked responsibly he would be good, and he had been.

"Say no more," he replied while digging in his pocket. It was as if he had been waiting for Havoc to ask him this question all his life, the way he had his paper, leaf and weed ready to roll up. Havoc just shook his head taking a seat. He wanted to scold him, but how could he? Right now he needed it, and Ivory was coming through with it. He watched as Ivory rolled up the perfect blunt, as if he rolled blunts for a living.

He pulled the lighter out his pocket, lit the blunt before taking a long drag from it then passed it to Havoc. Havoc kicked his foot on top of the coffee table and gave the blunt one look before putting it to his lips. He hadn't smoked in so long and he wanted to feel some kind of disappointment for himself. But he knew he needed it. His mind was running a million miles a minute and he just wanted it cleared, and that was where the weed came in. In silence, the two of them smoked the blunt until it was done. And before Havoc knew it, his eyes were getting heavy, which was all he wanted. He already knew in the back of his mind that this weed coma was gonna give him the best sleep of his life.

CHAPTER 3

BEAUTIFUL NIGHTMARE

"You can't possess people; you can experience them."

— LAUREN LONDON/ NIPSEY HUSSLE

Bonnie sat in her spacious bathtub that was filled with bubbles as she waited on her king to come home. He had been away for three days on a hit and was to be walking through the door any minute. After becoming a hundred million dollars richer, it had given them the upper hand on getting the business back and under control. It had been a month since killing Harper and not a single guilty bone lived in Bonnie. In fact, she was more at peace now than she had ever been. The love that she once had for Harper had switched like a light and quickly turned into hate. Although love and hate fell hand in hand and required an abundant amount of energy, Bonnie refused to give her any more. So she just allowed the memory of her deceased ex-best friend to fall to the back of her mind and kept it pushing. It had been easier than she thought it would be, but a great deal of her distraction came from Biz. They had come up and were living their lives accordingly.

The war wasn't over. They were on their toes, because they knew Havoc would retaliate, just the when and where was the real question. In fact, they were shocked that he hadn't attempted yet. They weren't sure what the holdup was, but they both were on their A-game.

Bonnie winced as she felt a contraction coming on. Being pregnant wasn't the easiest thing in the world. She had thought it would be a walk in the park which it was, but this last month was dragging for her. The size of her stomach went from a small bulge to the size of a watermelon. With Doc checking on her every two weeks, she knew her baby was fine. Although she couldn't go on hits just yet, she had learned to occupy herself by ordering gender neutral baby clothing and décor.

She had actually grown tired of seeing yellow, green, and grey. She was ready to have her baby in her hand so she could buy things accordingly.

Bonnie rose out the tub and washed her body off before stepping out the bath. After wrapping her plush white robe on, she picked up her phone, realizing that she had missed calls from Biz and dialed him back.

"Hey baby daddy," she teased through the phone, knowing that he hated when she called him that.

"Keep playing with a nigga, and I'mma show you what a real baby-daddy is," he answered.

"Yea aight nigga, and I'mma show you what a bitter baby mama is," Bonnie said laughing. Their relationship had become nothing but jokes and happiness. Being in a committed relationship was like a breath of fresh air for the both of them. They were learning more and more about one another every day and although most of the time they were happy, it was because when shit was bad between the two of them both of them secretly hurt. They had become one and didn't know what to do without the other.

"I'm on my way home ma, you need anything?" he asked like he always did. Biz was tough but for Bonnie, he was soft. He was smitten, he was her errand boy and he didn't complain. She was his queen and she was carrying his baby and he wanted her comfortable at all times.

Just as Bonnie was about to tell him that she could use a strawberry milkshake, a sharp pain in her abdomen caused the red flags in her mind to flash.

"Biz, I need help," she said as she began to feel a wave of dizziness come over her. She shook her head from side to side and for her that did more damage than she thought. At this point, she felt like the room around her was spinning, and like she would pass out any minute. She took a seat on the bed trying to recollect her thoughts while also trying to listen to what Biz was saying, but to no avail was her mind cooperating with her.

"Ahh!" Another sharp pain caused her to double over, causing her phone to fall to the ground. Worry instantly took over her as her eyes landed on a pool of blood between her legs. She opened up her mouth to call out for Biz but no sound came out; instead, she was met with another wave of dizziness. "My baby," she whimpered before the dizzy sensation took her out.

* * *

Biz threw his phone down in frustration knowing that something was wrong with Bonnie. He could hear the tone in her voice, and it tugged at his heart. He dodged traffic doing 90 mph in a 50 mph zone trying to get home to her. He was less than five minutes away and even that was too much for him. "Siri, call Doc," he said trying to get his nerves in check. He waited patiently as the phone began to ring through his earpods.

"Yo," Doc answered on the second ring.

"Meet me at the crib, something wrong with B," Biz said while still swerving through traffic and off the highway.

"Copy."

He hung up the phone and ran the few red lights that led to his house. As Biz pulled up to the driveway, he threw the car in park and hopped out running to the door. Although everything appeared normal and in place, he was suspecting the worst. It had become his way of thinking. It could've been Havoc and for that reason he took extra measures, pulling the Glock he had on his waistband and cocking it back leading a bullet in the chamber. He was ready to pop off if need be.

He rushed up the stairs taking them three at a time, rushing straight to their bedroom. The puddle of blood that Bonnie laid in made his heart sink and it was the first time he ever felt anything like it. The first thing he did when he rushed over to her was see if she had a pulse. He had never been so grateful in his life to actually feel a pulse. It was faint but it was there. He scooped her body into his arms and rushed down the stairs. He knew with the amount of blood that she was losing that if he didn't act fast and deliver their baby, there would be no baby. It was a chance he wasn't willing to take. He laid her on the kitchen floor and began grabbing kitchen appliances that would help him to improvise. His knowledge in the medical field was being put to the test at this very moment as he scrambled around getting what he needed to start. Doc was on his way and he knew he would be there ready to assist.

In a pot beside him was scorching hot water with scissors, a knife and rag. He began to concentrate as he counted the inches of where he would start her c-section with his finger. He grabbed the knife and hesitated for a minute. In that same minute Doc came rushing through the door. He took one glance around at the situation at hand and the amount of blood beneath her and gave Biz a nod, knowing already what it was he was about to do. Biz was doing exactly what he would've been doing if the roles were reversed. That was all the reassurance that Biz needed as he brought the knife down onto her lower abdomen. While he created an incision, Doc rushed over dropping his duffle bag full of medical supplies, instantly running her a general anesthesia. Although Bonnie was passed out without the anesthesia, she could feel every inch of pain that Biz was inflicting on her.

Biz continued to go to work cutting through layers of skin. When he finally got through, he moved to the side letting Doc do his thing. Just as fast as Doc's hands went in, they came out all covered in blood with a wailing baby.

"WAHHHHHH!" The piercing scream of their bouncing baby girl startled Biz for a minute as he adored her every feature. Although she was covered in blood, he could see the beauty in her already. A spitting image of her mother, he had never experienced love at first sight, but he was sure this was what it felt like. He was speechless.

"Take her," Doc said as he kept his eyes on Bonnie. He was in his zone and something wasn't right. He cut her umbilical cord as Biz grabbed a kitchen towel wrapping his baby girl in it. The minute the baby was out of his hands, Doc's hands began to maneuver inside of Bonnie again, and this time what he felt was a surprise to him.

"FUCK!" he said to himself out loud causing Biz to take his attention from his baby to Doc.

"Wassup?" he asked in an unsure tone.

"I don't know how the fuck I missed this shit."

Biz's brows furrowed together trying to see what exactly Doc was fussing about. Before he could ask again what was wrong, Doc's hand was coming out of her and so was another baby. Except this one was a boy and he was different. He wasn't wailing like his sister had been.

Twins? Biz thought to himself, confused. This was the one thing he had never expected, and it was happening. He stood there in shock as Doc sat there in panic. The baby didn't have a pulse and he was determined to get one.

"Pass me something to lay him on!" Doc instructed. And Biz obliged without asking any questions. He watched as Doc used his suction clearing the baby's airway then began to do CPR.

"WAAAAH!" he screamed, taking his first breath into the world. And the minute Doc heard it relief took over him, but there was no time. He turned from the baby and back to Bonnie, seeing that she was losing so much blood. He began to close her up and get her cleaned up while Biz tended to his children. In a matter of minutes, he went from a man with no kids, who pretty much couldn't have kids, to a father of two. After getting them cleaned up and dressed, he laid them in the crib that Bonnie had gotten for them and rushed back down to Doc.

Doc was wiping Bonnie's body down with a rag trying to get her cleaned up. "She lost a lot of blood bro, right now we at a waiting game. There's a pulse but it's faint. She's been through a lot and ain't no telling when she gon' get up. I gotta bring the rest of my medical stuff here. If I'm not mistaken, her brain is hemorrhaging."

Biz walked over taking the rag from Doc and cleaned Bonnie, nodding his head and taking in all the info that one of his best friends was telling him. The news was like a ton of bricks slapping him in the face. He was hearing everything Doc was saying but he didn't wanna hear it. He wanted Bonnie to wake up not now, but right now. She had just given him the best gifts in the world, and he owed her his life. All he wanted to do was give her the world. Losing her was gonna be the biggest L he took in his life and he couldn't afford it. He had just gotten used to the thought of being with a woman and learning how to love, and he wasn't ready to let her go. He needed her, their kids needed her, and that alone he felt was enough.

CHAPTER 4

ALLY

"Friends ask you questions, enemies question you."

— CRISS JAMIE

"Aye man, can I see these blue Retro 12's in a size 13 for kids?" Ivory asked the store salesman in Footlocker as he and CJ browsed the wall for shoes. Just as Ivory had thought, CJ changed. He talked less than he usually did. In fact, it was so bad that he only spoke when he was spoken to. Harper's death had taken a toll on him. When her life was taken from her a piece of CJ left as well. Ivory knew exactly how CJ felt. He himself had felt that same exact way when he witnessed his parents' death in cold blood. It was a sight that would leave any kid scarred for life. A sight that was etched in his mind and forever would be. Although his last memory was gruesome, that memory kept them alive to him. It had been years since his parents' passing, but the memory was still fresh. His mother's vibrant smile and his father's hearty laugh could never be forgotten. It was the one feature of the both of them that he loved the most.

He watched as the salesman came back with the shoe, and gave him a head nod silently thanking him before taking a seat beside CJ. "You like these?"

CJ nodded his head, but his facial expression didn't change not one bit. It was just blank; it had become a permanent look on him. It was as if he had forgotten how to smile, laugh, talk, or show any emotion.

Ivory was trying his hardest to cheer up the young boy but he knew the deal. He had been this kid once, and although it hadn't been this bad for him, everyone coped differently, and this was CJ's way of coping. He had been stuck by CJ's side while Havoc was trying to track down Bonnie and Biz. Just like that, it was as if they had been gone in the wind. There was no trace of them and even though it was pushing on two months, Havoc didn't stop. He needed to even the score. Bonnie had taken someone from him, and it was only right that he paid her back the favor. But no matter how far and wide he looked, it was as if they had been wiped clean off the earth, but Havoc knew good and well that wasn't the case. He could feel her presence and that she wasn't too far and he wasn't going to stop until he found them.

"Aight man, let's go pay for them." Ivory closed the sneaker box and walked over to the register, paying for the shoes and handing the bag to CJ. They had a long day as it was. Today was the last day of school for CJ and Ivory just thought he would treat the boy by taking him sneaker shopping because of his passing grades. He was unsure of how CJ did it, but he did. Hoping that a fresh pair of kicks would cheer CJ up maybe, but it was apparent that CJ didn't care about the sneakers, the one thing in this world he cared about, he couldn't have.

As they stood outside of the sneaker store waiting for their Uber to arrive, CJ looked up to the sky where the sun was shining and shook his head before bowing it down. As if he was defeated. "Your mom is up there CJ, and she is watching over you. You can't see her, but she can see you," Ivory spoke, already knowing the thoughts that were running through his head.

CJ didn't say a word but Ivory could tell that he heard his words loud and clear because he picked his head up.

Once their Uber pulled up, Ivory opened up the door letting CJ in before taking a seat beside him. They both looked out the windows as the country music from the radio played. Ivory looked at CJ who was still staring out the window, and grabbed his hand squeezing tightly. With his other hand he pulled out his phone to shoot Havoc a text.

Ivory: **BLACK SEDAN, MORSE RD**

He text, while adding a screenshot of the car info from his Uber app. Something wasn't right, and he could feel it. The vibe was off. He could've easily taken the pocket knife he had in his pocket and slit the driver's throat, but the only thing that stopped him was CJ. He had seen enough, and Ivory didn't want to add to it. His phone began to buzz, and it was Havoc.

Havoc: **PLAY IT COOL. OMW!**

Ivory sat back following instructions, acting oblivious to what was going on. He snuck two looks at the driver who seemed to be more scared than Ivory, but he didn't say a word. Instead, he pulled out a paper and pencil from CJ's book bag that he was carrying and wrote a note on it passing it to CJ.

When this car stops, I want you to run as fast as you can, as far as you can.

CJ just nodded his head and for the first time, Ivory was happy that he wasn't his old self. The old CJ would've asked a million and one questions and that would've gotten them caught up.

About two minutes later they were in a back alley with dumpsters and trash everywhere. The driver looked in the rearview mirror before getting out. Ivory stayed seated not moving a muscle, until his door swung open. His mouth opened in shock as he stared into the eyes of a man he thought was dead. He had thought that maybe Bonnie or Biz was up to this, but now it was clear that this was a hit gone wrong.

Ivory couldn't believe it as he stared into the eyes of Benny Lays, his last test kill, and he couldn't believe it. He knew he was a dead man walking. "CJ RUN!" he yelled, and that was all it took for little CJ to take off with lightning bolts under his ass. Benny just stared at CJ as he took off running. It wasn't CJ he was after anyhow so he couldn't care less where the young boy went.

He focused his attention back to Ivory while giving him a menacing stare, but Ivory seemed unbothered by it and returned the glare. He already knew what was next. He was about to meet his maker and although deep in his heart he knew he wasn't done doing what he had to do on this earth, he didn't show Benny that. "Who the fuck sent you lil' nigga?!" he asked while picking Ivory up from the collar of his shirt.

"Fuck you! I ain't no snitch bitch," Ivory replied. He knew the game well enough to know that whether he told or not, he was a dead man, and plus he would never give Havoc up, so he was willing to go out like a G.

Benny shook his head from side to side while pulling his gun out his waistband. "Wrong answer lil' nigga." Just as he placed the gun in front of Ivory's chest, Ivory looked him square in his eyes waiting for him to deliver his fate, but the sound of the hammer of Havoc's gun caused Benny to let Ivory go.

"Benny, long time no see," Havoc spoke, taking two steps forward.

"What the fuck is going on Hav?" Benny replied while turning his gun from Ivory to Havoc.

"Is that any way to greet an old friend?" Havoc asked as he tucked his gun away and raised his hand in surrender mode. After staring for an extra two minutes, Benny tucked his gun away. He and Havoc both began taking steps towards one another.

"Man, a nigga don't know who's an enemy and who's a foe," Benny spoke up as he gave Havoc a low five and they embraced one another in a brotherly hug. Havoc nodded his head knowing exactly what Benny was speaking on. After all, he was the mastermind behind his hit. But he decided he would just play along.

"A nigga know exactly what you talking about. Motherfuckers been dropping like flies, no thanks to this lil' nigga," Havoc said while pointing at Ivory. Ivory stayed still returning the glare that Benny was dishing out to him. Before Benny could ask any questions Havoc continued to speak. "So we all know that Biz offed Khalil shit. And a nigga wasn't fitting to be next. So B and I devised a plan to take the nigga out. I thought the nigga was dead, but obviously not. All along this nigga Biz been alive and he had someone else doing his dirty work. His plan was to take all of us out and start Dead Silence from scratch. That nigga was training this lil' nigga the game. One day I get to the crib and ole boy pointing a gun at me, but you know me. Stay ready ain't gotta get ready, so my shit was aimed right back at the lil' nigga. Long story short, he knew he ain't live his best life yet and wasn't ready to meet his maker. So he let me take him under the wing. From what I know, I was his last kill."

Benny shook his head from side to side; all of this took him by surprise. "Wassup with B?" he asked.

"From what I know, Biz handled her himself. The nigga in hiding and I'm just tryna get my hands on him to off him."

Havoc could see the steam coming out of Benny's ears as he planted the seeds to his next plan. He knew telling Benny this, he would now have an ally. And what was better than one person looking to kill Biz, was two.

"So this nigga was just out here double crossing everyone that was loyal?" Benny asked for reassurance. He couldn't believe his ears but what Havoc was saying sounded like the best explanation for the hit on his life. Not only had there been an attempt to end him, but this attempt happened in front of everyone that he loved. A slight bit of disappointment plagued him because he had always been loyal and never stepped on anyone's toes. He didn't want to believe what Havoc was saying but after word got out about Biz killing Khalil, anything was possible. It was clear that he had no loyalty. The only person he was loyal to was himself. He wasn't sure why Biz was out for blood but now it was time for his blood to be bled by the hands of Benny.

Havoc just shook his head from side to side, acting as if he felt betrayed the same way Benny felt but on the inside, he knew he now had someone else on his team and Biz wouldn't be able to hide forever. What was better than two eyes were four, and he knew for sure that Benny would be on the lookout for Biz. It didn't matter who got to him first. He just wanted him dead.

"Man I'mma make some calls, see what people know and get back to you on that," Benny said while giving Havoc another five and hug. He gave Ivory one last glare as he looked over Havoc's shoulder. "Watch that lil' nigga. That nigga gone be trouble, I can already see it," he warned.

Havoc let out a small chuckle while thinking 'if only you knew.' But he didn't say a word. He gave Benny one last departing head nod before turning to walk away. Benny watched as Havoc threw his arm around Ivory's shoulder and walked away with him. Benny meant just what he had said. Something about Ivory rubbed him wrong and it wasn't just the fact that he had tried to kill him, but he could see that Ivory was out for something; he was unclear on what exactly. He shook his head while taking off in the opposite direction. Ivory wasn't his problem anymore, Biz was, or so he thought.

CHAPTER 5

THE HELP

"When we give cheerfully and accept gratefully, everyone is blessed."

— MAYA ANGELOU

Biz walked down the baby aisle in the supermarket as he pushed his shopping cart, as he looked at the different types of baby formulas. He grabbed a few cans of regular formula that his son Cassidy seemed to drink with no problem. But his baby girl Cassie wasn't having it. She was bourgeois already which was where her nickname bourgeois mama came from. It had been a month since the birth of the twins, and there was nothing more Biz loved than being a father. He bonded with his children so well he knew which cry was for hunger, a dirty diaper, because they needed to be burped, and if they were sleepy. He knew his kids more than he knew himself, and he was proud of it. Bonnie still hadn't shown any progress and of course Biz was holding down the fort. He was not only taking care of their children, but he was taking care of her as well. He made sure to take care of her hygiene on a daily and was just as attentive to her as he was to their children. In fact, this was his first time away from them since they were born and he'd only left to restock on the things they needed, knowing that with Doc they were in good hands.

Doc had been coming by every day to check on them and Bonnie. Although they were premature, they were learning quickly and showing so much progress. They had started out with a feeding tube, but it was imperative to Biz that they learned how to suck their own bottle and within a week, they had both gotten the hang of it. Although the twins were showing progress, Bonnie, on the other hand, was still unresponsive. She had a steady heartbeat, but that was just it. Biz was doing everything that he could to be the best father he could be. It was important for him to be the father that he never had. He had faith that Bonnie would pull through when she was ready, and he didn't mind doing what he had to do while she was comatose. But right now, the world was on his shoulders as he scanned the wall of formula looking for the perfect one for his baby girl.

"Do you need any help?" a saleswoman asked after realizing the confused look on his face. He wanted to decline but knew that he really did, and the longer he stood there browsing at formula, the longer he'd be away from his children.

"In fact, I do. My son drinks these formulas with ease, but my lil' mama, on the other hand, vomits it up every chance she gets. It comes from her mouth and nose; the milk never stays down," he explained to the woman.

A bright smile came across her face. "Aww, you have twins?" she questioned. And Biz just nodded his head while looking at the other formulas. "I know just what your lil' mama needs," the woman added as she walked a little farther down the aisle, stopping directly in front of the organic baby formula. She grabbed one down from the shelf and passed it to him. "This should do her right. My daughter had the same problem when she was a baby."

Biz looked at the can, reading the words and ingredients off of it, and compared it to the milk that Cassidy drank and within a minute, he made the decision that both Cassie and Cassidy would be drinking the organic brand. It was healthier and had less pesticides and that alone was enough for him to put the other cans back and grab two dozen of the organic one.

"Thank you, Missy," he said looking at her name tag. The woman flashed him a smile. She was impressed by Biz and she didn't even know him. She had rarely seen men come in and shop for their children, they usually left that up to the mothers. But Missy had no idea that Biz situation was different. He was nothing like other men. He was a father before anything, and he took pride in it.

"You're welcome, are you a single dad?" she asked.

"Are you a single mom?" Biz replied almost instantly, like it was a reflex question, coming off ruder than he intended. He could tell that his question made her want to run and hide because he had offended her but instead, she replied.

"Yes, in fact, my husband died a few months ago, and I wasn't asking to be rude or to get in bed with you. I asked because I rarely see fathers in this aisle. But again, my fault. I will get out of your hairs."

As she walked away, a small amount of guilt ate at him. She had just helped him out pointing him in the right direction to help his children, and his attitude to her was a slap in the face. "Shit," he mumbled under his breath while walking after her. "I apologize if I came off rude. I'm not a single father, but I am a struggling father. My lady's health had been failing her, so I'm just a man tryna figure all this shit out," he replied.

Missy stopped in her tracks while giving him a sad look. She knew the feeling of being the only parent and knew exactly what Biz was going through. "I know that one baby is a handful and ain't no telling with two how much harder it could be. I'm actually looking for another part time job to make ends meet. So, if you ever feeling like you need a break or a nanny, I'm ya girl," she said flashing a small smile.

Biz nodded his head, knowing that he would probably never need her services but watched as she pulled out a pen from her shirt pocket and jotted a number down on one of his cans of milk. "Here's my number, don't hesitate to call. I know how big a man's ego could be. My husband had one of the biggest there was," she explained. Biz just gave her a small smile before walking away from her and to the register to pay for his things.

He had been away from his children and Bonnie for longer than he had liked, and he was ready to get back home to them.

* * *

Biz walked into his house as the sound of the Quran played through his home. It was peaceful just how he liked it. He had discovered that the melodic sound of the Ayatal Kursi made his children sleep more peacefully and longer. It could even stop their fussing. After he put all the things away, he headed up to the nursery and saw Doc with both babies in his hands in the rocking chair, rocking back and forth. He just shook his head. He was beyond grateful for Doc; he had fallen through time after time. And although he didn't need anyone, he knew that he was where he was right now because of Doc. Doc had saved his life and was a major part of it.

"You straight?" Doc asked as he rose slowly and quietly from his seat, careful not to wake up the twins.

"Yea, look at you man. This look suits you," Biz joked to his friend. Doc laid both babies in the crib while chuckling and shaking his head.

"Nah man, I'll leave the baby making to you. I'll be the cool uncle that spoils them."

Biz chuckled as well as they both walked out the room. Doc walked ahead of him and led him to Bonnie's room. "What's different?"

Biz was already a step ahead of him; the minute he walked into the room he noticed. "Brain activity," he said, flashing the smile that he was trying to hold back. But it was damn near impossible. To anyone else, brain activity may have not been a big deal but to Biz, it was. Bonnie was strong and he knew with giving her the time that she needed she would pull through. Now it was a waiting game, waiting to see when she would finally wake up from her sleep. He walked over to Doc giving him a hug. "Man, you been holding it down bro. I owe you my life," he said, knowing that no amount of money that he could pay Doc could actually repay him for the things he did. For the care that Doc took of the twins and Bonnie, he was making a doctor's salary payment daily. He was the only one Biz trusted with his family. Doc didn't need to work another day in his life if he didn't want to. Working for Biz, he had been afforded a luxury lifestyle.

"It ain't about nothing fam, keep doing ya thing," Doc responded as he pulled away. He had always been loyal to Biz and would forever remain loyal. It was more than a friendship; they had built a brotherhood that could never be broken. "I'mma check in with you tomorrow man, gotta wash this baby vomit off me," he joked and Biz chuckled, knowing exactly what he was talking about. When Cassie vomited, she was not only vomiting on herself but she made sure to get the person who was holding her as well.

He followed Doc down the stairs and towards the front door. "What you think about a nanny?" Biz asked when they got to the door. Doc looked at him with an unsure face.

"A nanny? Nigga what you know about needing a nanny?" Doc joked, unsure if Biz was serious. But the look on Biz's face said it all. "Do you need one? Are you ready to trust someone with your kids like that?"

Doc was asking the same questions that Biz had been thinking the entire time. "I don't know man, a nigga just tryna be the best father he can be. And don't nobody know how to be a better parent than a single mother tryna make ends meet," he responded, trying to get Doc to see the way that he was thinking about it.

"Man listen, if you think you need the extra pair of hands, go for it. But make sure to do your research. You got too much to lose," Doc explained, and Biz nodded his head because his friend was right. Doc opened the front door and just before he walked out, he asked another question. "She got a fat ass?" They both began to laugh at their stupidity.

"I don't know nigga, wasn't checking for it," Biz replied honestly. Doc gave him a look that said stop lying.

"Bonnie gon' off her shit if one hair is misplaced on them babies," Doc said with all seriousness.

"Nigga, I'll off her shit," Biz said, wiping the smile off his face getting slightly defensive. The thought of anyone harming his babies made him want to shield them from the world. He wished he could lock them in a castle and throw away the key. But that wasn't how it went. He watched as Doc got into his car and drove off before going into the house and in his office to do some research on Missy.

From the split second he met her, she seemed to have her shit together and know what she was doing when it came to children. Biz didn't need her to really watch the children because he was so engulfed and hands on with them. He more so needed her as an extra pair of hands around the house. Her hours would be short, but it was worth what he would pay. But before he made any decisions, he had to run his own background check on her and find out everything about her from who her great-grandparents were to her deceased husband. Biz couldn't slip up; he was a family man now.

He searched up the phone number she had written in his computer database, and everything about her pulled up including the names and images of everyone associated with her. From her family to her co-workers, it was all there.

Biz's brows came together as he shook his head. He couldn't believe it. Her husband was none other than the deceased Benny Lays. Biz knew that he had died at the hands of Havoc and had forgotten that Benny had a wife and child at home. He wanted to rid himself of the information, but he couldn't. He and Benny had it good and he felt like he could look out by hiring his wife and paying her well. The devil on the left shoulder was telling him don't do it and the angel on the right was telling him what if the roles were reversed and shit got bad for Bonnie? He knew he'd want someone to look out.

He rubbed his goatee, a bit frustrated not knowing what to do, but that didn't last long before the piercing hunger cry of Cassie came through the monitor that was in his office. He rose from his seat to tend to his child. Missy would have to wait. He was going to have to weigh out his options and sleep on it.

CHAPTER 6

HAUNTING PAST

"You realize that our mistrust of the future makes it hard to give up the past."

— CHUCK PALAHNIUK

"*Sis, everything is going just as planned and falling in place, like I thought it would. Armon and I have dotted our I's and crossed our T's. Once this shit is over with, me, you, and Ivory are gon' live in Hawaii. You thought y'all were spoiled now? Just wait. Y'all gon' have the world,*" Maverick said to his wife as she braided down their little boy's hair. Ivory couldn't help but to eavesdrop on the conversation. He didn't know what exactly they were talking about, but the idea of him having the world in the palm of his hands sounded like a fairytale.

Already, he never went without. Anything he batted his eyes at, he got. Being so young, he could tell that money wasn't an issue for his parents. After all, they lived in a mini mansion in the burbs. He was living every black boys' dream life and he loved every minute of it. He couldn't imagine living a lifestyle any less than what he was already living. He had been born with a silver spoon in his mouth and the word "no" just never sat well with him. Now as he listened to his parents, he knew that he would probably never in his life hear the word no again. "Alright Maverick, now when and where is all this supposed to be going down?" Isis asked as she finished up the last few braids in her son's hair. This was their routine every Sunday. Whereas most black families focused on Sunday dinner, in their house, Sunday was focused on hair. Isis made sure to retwist her and Maverick's dreads and rebraid Ivory's as well. To her, hair was very important, especially when it came to appearances. You could be dressed like a homeless man in the street but with neat hair, everything else could be overlooked.

"Armon texted me not too long ago saying that he is on his way. In fact, he should've been here by now," Maverick replied to his wife while shaking his head from side to side after looking at the time. Armon was late for everything and it was the one thing Mav hated the most about his best friend. He and Armon were like two peas in a pod. They had grown up struggling and promised themselves that their families would never know the struggle they knew. At the age of 17, they both had tried to get their hands dirty selling coke. But to them, playing the block wasn't worth it. They were up at wee hours of the morning trying to make a sale. And trying to differentiate real customers from police officers became too much. They had figured out that slanging drugs was easier said than done. All the work behind it wasn't worth it, and that was when they decided the drug game wasn't for them.

It was Maverick's idea that instead of slanging drugs, he would leave that to the other niggas on the block. What he and Armon would do was stick them up for their money. What started up as a quick and easy way for two kids to make a living and get some money in their pockets to impress women, turned into a permanent job. Once they had gotten started, they couldn't stop. It was too easy robbing niggas of their hard work. It was like taking candy from a baby. Armon and Maverick seasoned their skills, getting better and better with each robbery. After being in the game for fifteen years, Maverick was ready to do the biggest bust of his life so he could get out the game. Every time he went on a lick, he had to make sure that he made it home to his family every night. He was their rock and he knew he had to continue being that for the rest of their lives. Isis and Ivory had grown accustomed to their luxury lifestyle and Maverick was determined to be done with that business, as well as being set for life.

"You know Armon better than anyone in this world. That man is fashionably late for everything. He's probably ironing one of his shirts, you know the nigga gotta be crisp every time he steps out," Isis teased, reading her husband's mind already. They had been married for ten years and with time, they became able to read one another's mind. "Ivory, I'm done baby. Now what you are going to do is clean up all these toys in my living room while I run your bath water," Isis instructed.

"Okay Mommy," Ivory said, getting up from his seat and going straight to the mirror to see his hair. He looked at the Iverson braids that his mother did, and a smile came across his face. Nobody in the world could braid better than his mother. Or at least that was what he thought. He began to gather up his toys while staring at his mother who was now massaging her husband's shoulders.

"I'm calling him now; this nigga is ridiculous," Maverick said, shaking his head. As soon as Maverick pulled his phone out his pocket to call Armon, Ivory headed straight up the stairs to his room to put his toys away. He had been taught that while they were on the phone he was to always be in a different room. They didn't want him to know about their business and it was a way to keep his innocence. They had only wanted him to know what they taught him.

As the phone began to ring in Maverick's ear, he could hear Armon's phone ringing in the house. It didn't take him long to figure out what was going on as he threw his phone down to the floor and began to jet up the stairs to get Ivory with Isis on his heel. It was a set up and he didn't care about himself at this moment. The two most important people in his life were what mattered most.

As he stepped into Ivory's room, the sight of his son being held at gunpoint by a masked stranger was enough to make his knees weak. "He's just a boy," Maverick said with defeat in his tone. This moment right here was the weakest Isis and Ivory had ever seen him. Seeing his father this way caused tears to roll down Ivory's face. He could feel that everything in his life would be different from this day forth. The fear in his parents' eyes told it all.

"Please, let them go. I'll give you anything you want," Maverick pleaded.

"That is exactly what your best friend said," the gunman said. It was a woman and it was apparent that the voice of a woman had shocked both Maverick and Isis. That was all Isis needed to hear as she took two steps forward to the gunwoman.

Click

The sound of her pulling the trigger went off and Isis stopped dead in her tracks and her heart began to sink. "I love a little game of Russian roulette, don't you? Come on," she teased.

"Ice, stop," Maverick said, knowing that his wife would try taking her chances. There was no telling when the gun would go off and she silently prayed that she got to the gunwoman before it went off. She saw it as this woman would try to kill her son regardless and if she could save him, she would with her dying breath. Tears began to flow from her eyes as she took another step towards them.

Click

Click

Click

The sound of the gunwoman pulling the trigger was beginning to sound like torment to everyone in the room. "STOP ISIS! JUST FUCKING STOP!" Maverick yelled, causing her and Ivory to jump slightly. This was the first time since they had been together that Maverick had raised his voice to her. At this point, tears were running down his face as well. He feared with every step she took that their son would be dead. He didn't want to live in a world without his wife and son. He had experienced a life with them and didn't know if he would be able to breathe the same without them. He knew that with every step that she took she was playing the devil's advocate.

Just one more step and I got that bitch, Isis thought to herself. Just as she began to take that step, she flashed Ivory a smile.

BANG!

A gunshot went off straight through Isis' head. The blood from her brain splattered all over Ivory as shock covered his face.

"NOOOOOOOOOOOOOO!" Maverick yelled. He began to run towards his wife but before he could reach—

BANG!

Another shot went off causing his body to lay lifeless right beside his wife.

Tears began to fall from Ivory's eyes, but he didn't say a word. He knew he was next. The sight of all the blood made him shudder. His mother's once perfect face was now nonexistent. He wanted to scream, shout, and fight but he knew it was of no use. They were gone and it wouldn't bring them back.

"You sure do know how to make a grand entrance bruh," the masked lady said. "I'm glad you came in when you did 'cause I was two seconds from beating her ass," she added.

"The safe is in the car, start it up. I'll handle the lil' nigga. The house

is doused with gas already. One match and this bitch gon' be up in flames," the masked man said.

The woman nudged Ivory's body to her partner, but his eyes didn't leave his parents. It was the last time he would see them, and he was still in shock that they were now corpses.

After about two minutes, the masked man grabbed Ivory, throwing him over his shoulder, before lighting a match and shooting a stray bullet into the house for sound effect. He walked out the backdoor and placed Ivory on his feet and looked him in his eyes. "Run! And don't look back," he told Ivory before walking away.

Ivory had no idea what to do. He was only five years old. The only thought that crossed his mind was to run back into the house and die along with his parents but even at five years old, he now had a vendetta. Although the gunman had saved his life, he vowed that he would hunt and kill him, for killing his parents. Those eyes he would never forget, not even in his wildest dreams.

As the gunman got into the car with his partner, she drove off the premises while snatching off her mask. "Damn nigga, what took you so long?" Bonnie asked her brother.

"Just drive," Havoc responded. It was their first real hit before they got their Dead Silence tattoos and meanwhile, Bonnie couldn't wait. Havoc couldn't help but to think about the young boy's life he saved.

Havoc jumped out his sleep with sweat coming down his face. He had ruined Ivory's life and now he felt like he was ruining CJ's. The silhouette of a person standing in front of his room door caused him to grab his gun that he slept with underneath his pillow and pull the hammer back. In a swift motion, he turned on the light and aimed his gun.

A bloodied CJ stood before him and instantly panic began to set in. He put the gun down and dashed up from the bed examining CJ's body. He stopped in his tracks after realizing that the smell of the blood wasn't from a human being. He had killed enough to know what human blood smelled like. "CJ, what happened?" he asked with a little confusion.

CJ said nothing. He just grabbed Havoc's hand and directed him out the room and into the foyer. Havoc looked on in shock as he witnessed the dead racoon in his home. He had so much to say but not a single word escaped. One thing for sure and two things for certain, this wasn't a good sign.

CHAPTER 7

DADDY SHARK

"There is a spark in us of something good, something right and beautiful."

— RICK TUMLINSON

Biz sat beside Bonnie's bedside while reading Murderville by Ashley and Jaquavis out loud to her. It had been two months of brain activity and Bonnie still hadn't opened her eyes and Biz was feeling helpless. There was no one in the world who understood what he was feeling, except the character Ashai from his book. Bonnie was his Liberty, his weakness. As he finished up a chapter, he inserted a bookmark before grabbing the brush on the nightstand and brushing her hair. This became a daily routine for him. He knew that Bonnie would have a fit If he let her just lay there as months flew by and didn't keep up with her appearance. Before, the twins had occupied most of his time, but now that Missy had become an extra pair of hands for him, everything ran smoother. She knew his children as well as he did. She knew the cry, the fuss, everything that a mother should know about their child, she knew.

The kids took a liking to her, her first week working with them. It was going on a month and it was safe to say they were attached to Missy. When she put them down to do other work around the house, they fussed. They had her wrapped around their little fingers, and she was spoiling them rotten. Biz was unsure if that was a good or bad thing. His kids were attached to someone who wasn't their mother. He knew if Bonnie was alert that she wouldn't be having it. In fact, she would probably be hosting a double funeral for Biz and Missy. The thought of it caused Biz to chuckle to himself. He missed his lady and there was no denying it. Although her physical form was there, he missed everything else about her that he had taken for granted. He had spent so long trying to act like there was nothing between them that he regretted it. He wanted to make the hands of time rewind, so that every minute that he had spent avoiding her and the spark between them, trying to convince himself that they were no good for one another, like two ticking bombs waiting to explode, they could've explored one another.

A soft knock sounded at the door, and he stopped brushing her hair. He knew it was Missy. He had restricted her from certain areas of the house to contain his privacy, and she respected his boundaries. He kissed Bonnie on the forehead before standing up and admiring her beauty. There was no one more beautiful in the world to him. If it wasn't for all the machines that she was hooked up to, she would be assumed to be sleep. He walked to the door letting himself out and instantly connecting eyes with Missy. She had become a useful pair of hands around his house, and he was grateful. At first, he had considered not hiring her because of his past business with her husband. But knowing that Havoc had terminated everyone in the company, even Benny, the one person who actually had a family to tend to, his conscious told him otherwise. He had put Bonnie in her shoes and knew that if it ever came down to it where times were hard for her, he would've wanted Doc to look out for her or anyone for that matter. He didn't bring up her husband nor did he act like he knew him.

"How is she?" she asked in a concerned voice.

"She's straight," Biz replied, not wanting to discuss Bonnie. She wasn't a topic to be discussed with anyone except Doc.

"Okay, well both of the munchkins are out cold. That's what a warm bath and bottle will do," she replied as she turned to head down the stairs with Biz right behind her. Her work for the day was done and she wasn't ready to go home. With every step she took, her big ole booty hypnotized him. She had the kind of behind that made even women stare and wonder if it was real. With the jiggle in every step, Biz knew it was real. She had the kind of ass that made any nigga's dick hard and want to put it in her. So, the hard-on he was sporting through his grey sweats wasn't because he was attracted to her, but because he was a man.

The two walked into the kitchen and Missy grabbed two wine glasses and the bottle of vintage wine that she had found a few days back in the cabinet. She could tell that Biz wasn't a drinking, mingling, partying kind of man. His cabinet was full of wines that had never been opened. She lifted the bottle for Biz to see, silently asking if it was okay to open, and he just shrugged his shoulders and took a seat at the island. He usually didn't mix business with pleasure; he had learned his lesson with Bonnie. Bonnie had been his one exception for a lot of things. No one could compare and he wasn't trying to find out if anyone could. Missy did her job and went about her business. But today she was different. She had fixed up her hair, and Biz noticed the light makeup that she wore but didn't need. He didn't know what it was that had her in a different mood and didn't really care to find out. He was in the comfort of his own home and knew that if shit went bad, it would be to her disadvantage. He didn't mind having a little company; he was lonely and confined to his house. Talking to the nanny wouldn't kill him.

He watched as she poured them both a glass of wine, it was of habit. He didn't drink anything from anyone unless he saw them pour it with his own eyes. She walked over to him handing him his glass and standing between his legs as she raised her glass to a toast. "To new beginnings."

Biz looked at her letting their eyes reconnect as he toasted his glass onto hers. "To new beginnings."

They both put the drinks to their lips and downed it as if they were in competition, their eyes never breaking contact. As they both sat their glasses down, their staring competition continued. Biz was trying to read her as she was trying to read him. As he scooted his stool back to create space between them, Missy took a step forward closing the gap again. This time she reached her hand slowly placing it on his gunshot wound on his face and caressed it slowly, as if it would still hurt him. "How'd you get this?" she asked softly, already knowing that Biz was closed off and wouldn't tell her, but it was worth a shot. She was intrigued by him. Since the first day she laid eyes on him. She didn't care that he belonged to another woman. He was the type of man that her husband once was. Little did she know, her husband had followed Biz's every step to be like him. Biz thought of answering the best way he knew how, but he didn't. Instead, he grabbed her hand and held it in his palms before scooting back once more and standing up.

She took another step towards him, so desperately not wanting to be any more than two feet away from him. Being around him, she felt safe, and a connection. And it didn't matter that he tried to fake it like he didn't feel it as well, but she knew. She laid her head on his chest knowing that this wouldn't last for long, and she squeezed her eyes shut not wanting to pull away, but of course he did.

"Goodnight Missy," he said while walking away from her. He headed upstairs to the twins' nursery as guilt plagued him. He hadn't done anything wrong physically but emotionally, they connected. When she had touched his face, he saw in her eyes that she cared, he felt her sincerity. It was like never before. He hadn't been out much since being shot but when he did, he got stares from everyone who walked the streets, but it seemed like the minute he met Missy she didn't judge him, not even a little bit. She saw him, she saw way past the surface, she tangoed with his soul. He felt like he was betraying Bonnie even though he wasn't doing anything. He knew that everything was all wrong, but he would never admit to how he felt with Missy and he wasn't sure if he was doing himself a favor or lying to himself.

As he stepped foot in the nursery, he took a deep breath before walking over to his children. He looked at his son and daughter who were his spitting image. There was no doubt in his mind that they were his. A DNA test could tell him they weren't, and he'd say it was a lie. Their looks had changed so much in the three months since they were born, and it seemed like every day he was looking at baby Bonnies or baby Bizzes. He shook his head at how fast time flew, and the fact that it had already been three months. An empty feeling came over him, because he knew that his kids needed Bonnie, and she was missing out. He just wanted her to wake up and meet the two beautiful babies that she had pushed out and get to know them. He had everything down pat when it came to them but the one thing he could never do was be their mother or even try to replicate her. Yea, they enjoyed Missy, but it was only because she was a mother and naturally women were nurturers. His children had sensed it and liked it because their mother was unable to deliver this feeling.

CHAPTER 8

BAD BOY, BAD BOY

"Good boys are no fun, and bad boys are no good."

— MARY J. BLIGE

> *"My hunger is equal to my struggle*
> *I came from nothin'*
> *Grindin' then I made it to something*
> *The age of a youngin'*
> *Started handing and bangin' and hustlin'."*

The sound of G Herbo played through the club as Havoc sat back with his shades on as Vee danced in front of him with her ass out, shaking it like her life depended on it. The strip club was booming for it to be a Thursday night, but it was obvious that the place wasn't full of your average Joe's who had 9-to-5 jobs. It was full of hustlers. All the money being thrown and there wasn't a clean dollar in sight. But that was what the strippers liked, dirty money.

"Let's get up out of here," Vee whispered into his ear, sensing that something was wrong. Havoc's vibe was off compared to the regular him. She knew Havoc well enough and one thing that made shit better for him was some good pussy, and she could deliver. He nodded his head and stood to his feet, taking one last look at the scenery, and walked out.

As he stood outside he passed his ticket to valet and waited on Vee to come out. He was sure she was somewhere in the backroom counting the money she made and putting on the little bit of clothes that she had come to work in. Havoc knew he hadn't been himself lately and just felt that maybe, just maybe Vee could fill that void. He knew he was fooling himself; Vee couldn't fill anything within him. All she was good for was a quick nut.

A mixture of not being able to find Biz and Bonnie along with Harper's death made him hot. He was less reasonable than he had already been. All his eggs were in one basket as he waited for Benny to get back to him with some information. He pulled the blunt from behind his ear and sparked it up, taking a long pull from it. This had become his regular. A blunt seemed to always help him escape his reality. The reality that he was raising two boys with no idea how to. Shit, he had never been raised before and Ivory was turning out to be a miniature version of him, and he knew in the back of his mind that he was fucking up Ivory the same way Biz had fucked him up. The reality of the dent Biz and Bonnie had put in his pocket when he got CJ back settled in. Although he wasn't fully broke, and his lifestyle remained the same as it always had been because he wasn't a flashy nigga, he couldn't accept the fact that anyone had gotten away with his hard-earned money. And the reality of Harper's death was the biggest reality he tried escaping. Although time after time he told himself what he and Harper had was nothing, his emotions said otherwise. He couldn't shake her from his system.

He watched as valet pulled up with his car and went in his pocket to tip him, but instead, Vee put her hands over his stopping him. "I got it," she said as she pulled out one of the crumbly twenties she had in her bag and passed it to the guy. Once they were both secured in the car,

Havoc sped off while playing J. Cole's "Middle Child." He and Vee sat in silence and she could feel the built-up tension in the car. She knew better than to ask him any questions; if he wanted to talk, he would. So, she did what she had been wanting to do all night. She pulled his dick out and instantly placed it in her mouth. She loved Havoc's dick. To her it was perfect in length and girth, and he knew how to work it. She bobbed her head up and down as he sped down the freeway. The adrenaline rush from feeling the car switch lanes left and right made her wet. She put her leg up on the chair and with her other hand began playing with her clit. Just as the car came to a stop, they were both releasing their first orgasm. Vee made sure to lick up every drip of semen. It was her favorite part of giving him head; she got a chance to fill herself up with him.

"Fuck me," she whispered, and that was all that needed to be said. She climbed to the back seat and tooted her ass as high up in the air as she could, and he followed. For the first time in the years they had been messing with one another, Havoc had never went in her raw, but today was the day and Vee silently hoped and prayed in her head that this one time would be enough for her to get pregnant. He grabbed her waist pumping in and out of her as silent moans escaped her lips. She was unsure if she was experiencing pain or pleasure, but it didn't matter because she wanted it all from him. Havoc pulled his dick out her pussy and slid it right in her ass without a warning. Vee wanted to run but she wouldn't dare. She wanted Havoc to have his way with her, proving that she was the girl for him. The pain quickly turned into pleasure and she played with her clit feeling a rush of another orgasm. With each grunt that Havoc let out, she knew that he was near orgasm as well. She threw her ass back onto him matching the rhythm of his thrusts. Then there it was, orgasm number two of the night. Vee laid on her stomach, out of breath as Havoc sat on his chair beside her. "That was amazing."

"I know," Havoc replied while pulling a wet wipe from beneath his seat, passing one to her and grabbing one for himself.

"Hav, I got someone who wants to meet you," Vee said with hesitation in her voice. Before he could even reply, he could feel the presence of someone else in his car. He grabbed his pistol that was underneath his seat and in one swift movement, he was pointing his gun at another stripper.

"What the fuck Vee!" he yelled as he grabbed the stripper's neck, squeezing hard enough to break it. She scrambled and fought, and Vee looked on in surprise. "You don't fucking know me by now ma? I will squeeze the fucking life out this bitch!"

"Havoc, just hear her out!!!" Vee yelled as she tried to loosen his grip on her friend. Havoc's temper was at a million right now. The fact that he had been slipping enraged him. This could've been anyone waiting to clap at him. He loosened his grip on the stripper and watched as she tried to catch her breath.

"My...name... is Cynthia," she said in between gasps. Havoc didn't care who she was and in five seconds, her brain was about to be splattered all over his car. He was unsure if he was madder at Vee or himself, but someone was gonna feel his wrath; his trigger finger was itching. "I know Biz," Cynthia said when she finally caught her breath.

That was music to Havoc's ears. BANG! He shot a hole straight through Vee's head without even looking at her. If she could allow a stripper to hide in his trunk, she was capable of letting a nigga who wanted him dead to do the same. She couldn't be trusted, and she had crossed a line.

"AHHHHHH!" Cynthia screamed as she watched her best friend's brain splatter all over the window of the car. She hadn't thought about how this plan could've backfired and now here she was scared for her life. Vee hadn't told her that this nigga was crazy. All she wanted was for him to hear her out. She threw her hands up in surrender mode, hoping that she wasn't next. "I... I'm...his daughter's mother," she stuttered in fear.

Havoc's eyebrows began to crease up, knowing that she was lying. Biz didn't have kids, except the one he and Bonnie were having, or at least that was what he thought. Cynthia could sense his uneasiness about the situation. And she had come prepared for this. She grabbed the pictures of her and Biz together, proving that she knew him.

"These are old," Havoc said as he stared at the picture.

"Nine years old to be exact," Cynthia added. "We had a baby together and he went ghost on me. No explanation, nothing. And I let it go at first but why should that nigga get an easy pass while I'm out here struggling as a single fucking mother? That nigga needs to pay. I been hearing that you and Benny looking for him and I am too," she explained. Havoc nodded his head somewhat believing her, only because she mentioned Benny and right now, she was scared for her life.

"I can't help you," Havoc answered while fixing himself up. He didn't know shorty from a can of paint and for all he knew she probably just wanted to be wrapped around the nigga Biz dick. She pulled her phone out her pocket desperately and dialed a number while putting the pone on speaker.

"Benny, it's Cyn. I'm with your friend Havoc. Back me up."

"Hav, her word is bond. Cyn and I go way back. I knew about her when they were dealing with one another. Ain't nothing worse than a woman scorned, she's an asset" Benny confirmed.

"Copy," Havoc replied and Cyn hung up the phone as a smile crept up on her face. "What do you want?" he asked, knowing that there was a reason other than the fact that he had walked out on her and a child that she was willing to team up with Benny and him.

"I want it all. You see my situation. A bitch is stripping to make ends meet. I know him well enough to know the nigga is living great. Shit, this the same nigga who moved me into a gated house when he found out I was pregnant. So, his pockets is deep and that's all I care about. The money. So y'all want him dead, I want his money. If anything, using me as bate would solve y'all problems. It's a win/win situation for us all. Benny go back to his family. You get your vendetta and I get the bread. We all gon' eat," she explained as if she had it all planned out.

Havoc knew what she was saying made sense, but it was gonna take a whole lot of more planning than she thought. Biz had slipped by once and he was determined that he wouldn't again and this time he didn't need any more casualties. "Where's your kid?"

"Somewhere safe. So, we doing this or what?"

Havoc climbed back to his front seat and started up his car. "What, you gon' stay seated in the trunk?" he asked as he began to drive. Cynthia was happy that he had cut her in on the deal but hated that Vee had gotten the short end of the stick. She looked over at all the blood in the seat and around the car and cringed. She wasn't built for killing. She was a bread chaser and that's it. She climbed over the chair sitting in the spot that Havoc had previously been sitting in, the only spot that was clean, and did the sign of the cross.

"I'm sorry Vee," she whispered to herself as two lone tears slipped out her eyes. She was happy to be getting back at Biz, but she was terrified of Havoc. He had shown her how ruthless he could be in the first thirty seconds of interacting with him. She knew he wasn't to be fucked with and made a mental note to tread lightly around him. He was a ticking time bomb just waiting to happen.

CHAPTER 9

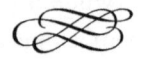

LOVERS AND FRIENDS

"Sometimes wanna be ya lover, sometimes wanna be ya friend, sometimes wanna hug ya hold hands, slow dance while the record spins."

— LUDACRIS

Missy and Biz sat on the floor with the twins admiring them while they had their tummy time. In a week they would be turning four months and Biz couldn't be happier. He was a changed man. His children brought out a side of him he didn't know he was capable of having. It had been three weeks since the connection between Missy and Biz and neither one spoke on it. The two of them refused to cross that line knowing that it would only complicate things in the end. After all, Biz was in a committed relationship. They avoided having a conversation about what happened so that it wouldn't make anything awkward. But they had built a friendship behind it. Biz knew Missy meant no harm, but he also knew he couldn't give her anything more than a friendship.

He wanted Missy around and Missy wanted to be around. Biz didn't know it but he was her high, her daily dose of crack to get her through the day. Just being around him made her feel like a new woman. She knew they would never be but the thought of them being everything she wanted made her feel good. Ever since her daughter's tragic birthday party, she hadn't been the same or felt the same. It was like Benny dying had sucked the life out of her. But Biz, that damn Biz brought that feeling back to her. He lighted up a spark within her that she thought was gone forever.

After Benny's death, she had stopped caring about her appearance. And her wardrobe had begun to consist of only work uniforms. But now, she was back at it. Her hair was done once a week, her light natural makeup that she used to make her face glow had become her best friend, and she had begun dressing like a runway model. Biz had taken notice but didn't comment on it. It actually flattered him a bit, that not only did she see him with his visible flaws, but she was trying to gain his attention. The attention that he couldn't give. He didn't want to mislead Missy, because although she infatuated him, Bonnie had his heart. She was his equal and although Missy may have probably been his soulmate, he would do nothing but destroy her. and having someone as innocent and pure as her blood on his hands, he wouldn't be able to deal with. A friend was all he could be to her and it was all that he would give. Unbeknownst to him befriending her only made her feelings for him grow. And it was the simplest gestures, like pulling out her chair to sit, or opening a door for her letting her walk in first. The chivalry that he felt that every woman deserved was what Missy was flattered by.

She watched as he rolled Cassie over onto her back and began to play a game of peek-a-boo with her causing his baby girl to erupt in laughter. Her laughter only caused Biz and Missy to laugh as well. "You like that bourgeois mama?" He cooed as he swooped her up into his arms and held her in the air. He was showing Missy a side of him no one had ever saw, not even Bonnie. The way he let his guard down with his children was a turn on for Missy. It was the one thing she wished Benny would've done with their daughter. Memories like this were precious to children and it made them admire their parents even more. As she thought about Benny a sadness came over her. Her daughter had lucked out on a dad because of the life he chose to lead. He hadn't thought of the repercussions and how shit could come back and bite him in the ass. Her sadness began to turn into anger, because she knew in the end that it would affect her daughter entirely.

"What on your mind?" Biz as realizing the change in Missy. She tried to pull herself together, but it was no use, he knew something was up.

"Nothing, you are an amazing dad, and they are lucky to have a father like you," Missy said flashing a smile.

"You sure I'm amazing? The look on your face says otherwise. Shit the look on your face make a nigga feel like he doing everything wrong," he joked trying to lighten up the room. He could tell she was in her feelings and knew that with feelings came vulnerability.

Missy flashed him a smile before responding. "You aight!" And they both began to laugh. This was what he enjoyed about their friendship; the shit felt normal. He couldn't remember the last time he had felt a normal connection with someone who knew nothing about what he did for a living and someone who didn't look at him like a monster. In fact Missy was the first. He refused to get her tangled in his web. It was too sticky and too hard to get out of and she didn't deserve anything as complicated as that.

"Last one up the stairs gotta change the shitty diapers!" Biz joked while holding Cassie as if she were a football and running up the stairs.

"Unh unh!" Missy squealed laughing as she grabbed Cassidy up holding him close to her chest trying to catch up to Biz. All the commotion did nothing but make the twins laugh like they were tickled by the behavior of their father and nanny. Once Biz got to the top, he held Cassie up in the air like Rafiki did Simba in Lion King while sticking his face close to her behind smelling the booboo she made. Missy began laughing so hard that she couldn't catch her breath. Biz was happy to see that just that quick he was able to change her mood.

"Bourgeois mama, you go with Miss Missy, and fat man, you come to daddy," Biz said as they walked into the nursery and swapped babies. Missy just shook her head from side to side chuckling.

"Boy do you know how to cheat."

"Nah, girl don't hate the player hate the game, you was too slow, a nigga was running like Usain Bolt" Biz joked as he changed Cassidy's diaper.

"Usain Bolt my ass, you had a head start!"

"Okay, last one done changing the diaper is a rotten egg."

Missy began to laugh again. "Boy eff you!" she replied knowing that in this race she also had the short end of the stick. While she was stuck changing shit, he was changing piss.

"Done," Biz boasted once again, and Missy just shook her head from side to side as she slipped Cassie's diaper on.

"Cheater."

Biz just chuckled and laid Cassidy in his crib turning on his mobile. His kids were on a schedule thanks to Missy and he loved it.

When she got done with Cassie, she laid her in her crib as well doing the same thing and turning on the Quran to play softly. Both babies began to yawn; it was like they knew it was time for them to sleep. "Thank you," Biz said as he bent down and kissed Cassidy, then Cassie.

Missy just gave him a smile standing in front of him. She had grown attached to his kids and began to love them how she loved her own daughter but how did she express that to him without looking like a creep. Instead, she just replied. "You're welcome."

They stared at one another and Missy decided to just go for it. She stood to her tip toes and placed her lip on his. The softness of his lips made her pussy begin to cream. He pulled back like he had been burned by fire and Missy looked at him in surprise. Instead, she realized that she didn't have his attention, something behind her did.

She turned around and her mouth dropped to the floor as she stared in the eyes of the women whose man she was kissing on. "Pick ya jaw off the floor bitch, I'm back," Bonnie spoke while giving Missy a stare that could send her six feet deep.

Biz stared on and on in shock, not saying a word. He had never been so shocked in his life. It was as if she had awakened from the dead. He walked over to her and placed his hands on her face making sure that it was real. He had dreamt of this moment plenty of times and wanted to make sure that he wasn't dreaming right now. Bonnie gave him a stare that told him he wasn't getting out of what she had just seen so quickly, but he didn't care. He was happy that she was up and alert. He could feel her hesitance and knew he would feel her wrath but right now, he didn't care about that. He pulled her into a hug and wrapped his arms around her while placing his chin on top of her head. "Thank you, God," he whispered as he kissed her forehead.

She pulled away from him and turned her attention back to Missy. "Bitch you can step, or I can help you. You pick."

Missy just cleared her throat while looking at Biz who shrugged his shoulders. "Goodnight Missy, we'll see you tomorrow," he said, knowing that Bonnie wasn't gonna repeat herself one too many times. In fact, he was actually saving Missy and she didn't even know it.

"Doubt it," Bonnie added while grilling Biz.

Missy nodded her head and headed towards the door and stopped in her tracks and turned to Bonnie. "I'm so sorry," she whispered. Bonnie didn't say a word; instead, she looked at Missy like shit on the bottom of a shoe before walking away and heading to the cribs to see her babies. Biz followed behind her and wrapped his hands around her waist while tucking his face in the crook of her neck and inhaling.

"I missed you B."

Missy stared at the intimacy of the couple and felt stupid. How could she ever think she would have a chance with a man of Biz's caliber? She knew he was taken and she felt more stupid for the fact that she had kissed him. She had made herself look like a fool not only in front of him but also in front of his lady. She shook her head back and forth as she exited the house just hoping that she hadn't just cost herself her job. She needed the extra money and it wasn't only that. She felt like she needed to see Biz. He was the medication that the doctor hadn't prescribed her because they knew she would get addicted and here *she* was, moping and hoping that she would see him again. She knew if she didn't it wouldn't be anyone's fault but her own. She had made a move, and she had gotten caught. The way that Biz had embraced Bonnie made her heart drop. That right there was love and she knew she couldn't get between it. Missy took notice of it all, the way he looked at her, the way he touched her with gentleness. All ways that she had secretly wished that Biz would show her, he showed Bonnie. There was no competition between the two and it was obvious. Bonnie had Biz's heart and Missy couldn't compare.

She looked up at the window one last time and once again she was looking into the eyes of Bonnie who stood there with a smirk on her face as Biz stood behind her, holding her like she would vanish if he let go of her. Missy turned away as tears began to form in her eyes. In her thirty years of life she had never wished she was the next bitch until today.

CHAPTER 10

'TIL DEATH DO US APART

"I can accept failure; everyone fails at something. But I can't accept not trying."

— MICHAEL JORDAN

Benny sat in a trance thinking about how he had an extra chance at life. He remembered the day his life was supposed to be taken from him and still couldn't wrap his head around the chaos and how he pulled it off.

"Help!! Help my daddy!!" Benny heard his daughter Beatrice yell. He didn't know what was happening to his body but it seemed like it was shutting down on its own. Not able to move, talk or see he felt like his body was giving up on him as he hit the bottom of the pool. The fear in his daughter's voice made him want to shoot up like nothing was wrong but it seemed impossible. Not too long after he heard his wife Missy screaming at the top of her lungs while his body was being carried out the water.

"Call 911!" he heard a voice call out. Benny wanted to tell them all they were overreacting, but he was sure if they really were. Someone had just tried to take his life so his best bet was to act like he was dead. He could hear the cries from his daughter and wife and wanted to tell them everything was going to be alright, but it was clear that he couldn't guarantee it. He had put them at risk, but luckily, he was the only target.

"Missy I got him. I'll ride to the hospital with him. You just shut everything down. Send everyone home, you and Bee get in and stay in," Benny heard his right-hand man West say. Benny could hear the murmurs of all the family and friends that they had in attendance as they all wondered what had just happened. He knew they were assuming that maybe he had a heart attack or was going through a natural death, but Benny knew that wasn't the case. His health was A1 and he stood on top of it. Plus, he'd killed enough to know when someone was trying to kill him. The question was who, and a why would've been nice, but it wasn't needed.

He felt the paramedics lay him on a gurney and just laid still. He was concocting a plan in his head to make his death seem real. Someone wanted him dead, so he was going to be dead. If anyone knew he was alive that would only make the person come back and try again. But he wanted to do his research and be two steps ahead, killing the person who tried to kill him first. Like a game of tag, he didn't want to be it.

* * *

Once Benny was in the hospital room and the doctor finished examining him, he opened his eyes and was glad to see West. He decided to cut straight to the chase letting West know of his plan. "Someone tryna take me out, so a nigga gotta act like they did. You gotta tell Missy I'm gone."

West shook his head from side to side. "Come on Ben, you know Missy ain't going for that. She wanna see a body to make sure there ain't no pulse and if she up to it, you finna have a big ass funeral."

Benny chuckled at the thought of his wife 'cause he knew West was right. But he shook his head. "Come on, do me a solid. Shit, cremate me for all I care. She can't know. It's too dangerous and after it's all done, you should lay low too. If someone is after me, then they gon' be after you soon enough."

"Man, you gon' have Missy kill me; you know sis don't play about you. Nigga I'mma have to make this shit look good, so make that shit look good on your behalf as well," West replied, knowing that he was gon' help his mans out no matter the situation. Benny nodded his head as he thought of his next move.

Benny watched as the doctor stepped into the room and he wanted answers. "Doc, wassup, why a nigga passed out like that?" he asked.

The middle-aged Indian man looked over his glasses at Benny as he began pulling out the IV's in his arm and grabbing up his clothing to get dressed. "Mr. Lays, in your bloodwork I see that you consumed a large but not deadly amount of chloroform. If you would've drank an ounce more, you would've been dead," the doctor explained. He looked at Benny who nodded his head. But he didn't say another word about it. "It seems like you are feeling like yourself already, so I will have a nurse bring your discharge papers," he added, and Benny nodded his head.

He watched as West went into his pocket and pulled out a large band of money tucking it in the doctor's hand. "Doc, let's just say he was never here, okay?" The doctor didn't even look down into his hands. He knew he was holding retirement money in his hand and instead of saying another word, he tucked the money into his pocket and walked out the room.

West and Benny looked at one another and chuckled. "Shit, I thought I was gon' have to give the nigga another fifty bands, but I guess not," West joked. He stood to his feet as Benny finished putting on his clothing and walked to his friend, knowing that he wouldn't be seeing him for a while.

"Stay safe bro," West said while dapping Benny and pulling him in for a brotherly hug.

"You already know, watch over Missy and Bee for me man. I'mma be gone for a while so hold down the fort. You know I'm good for it," Benny replied.

West pulled away nodding his head. *"Without a doubt. Keep a nigga up to date on ya moves when you get settled. I'm about to lay low for a while too."*

Benny nodded his head one last time before walking out the hospital room and disappearing the way everyone thought he had.

Benny stared at the pictures in his hand that his informant had given him. Ever since he was presumed dead, he had made sure to try and keep a close eye on his wife and daughter. He wanted to make sure that whoever had targeted him wasn't targeting them next. His whole point of going into hiding was to keep them safe and he figured it had been working for the last few months, but as he now looked at the pictures of Missy and Biz, he was unsure what was going on. None of the pictures were intimate but just the interaction alone made his blood boil.

He knew his wife well enough to know when she was glowing and in these pictures, she was. He didn't want to imagine whatever it might've been going on between them. He was unsure if Missy knew exactly who Biz was, but he was 100% sure that Biz knew who Missy was.

Had they planned this? Was Missy in on the hit? Those were the questions that ran through Benny's mind as he stared at the pictures. Not one to act on emotions, he put the pictures down and began pacing the floor. He needed to get his mind right and figure out everything he could on what Missy was doing with Biz. He knew there was only one person that he could call that would find out what was going on with Missy, and it was no one other than his right-hand man West. Although they were laying low, right now wasn't the time. Images of Biz enjoying his woman the way he once did evaded his mind, making him squeeze his phone then throw it on the floor. He didn't want to think that his wife would cross him. She couldn't have. With his emotions at an all-time high, he grabbed a Cuban cigar and lit it while tapping. He didn't play when it came to his wife and daughter and just hoped that his suspicions were running wild because his wife was with the enemy. He was determined to get to the bottom of it, even if it killed him.

* * *

Missy kicked her legs in the air, frustrated at how stupid she could've been. Biz had text her giving her the day off and she didn't know if she was off for the day or off forever. Either way, she knew she had made her bed and she would have to lay in it. Although her job was on the line, she couldn't get over how beautiful Bonnie was. It was the first time she laid eyes on her and for someone who had declining health, she looked damn good. Jealousy surrounded her as she thought of the way that Biz had been with her. He had been so calm and gentle with her, showing Bonnie everything that Missy had wanted from him. She had begun to think Biz was incapable, but that wasn't the case. He just wasn't interested in her and it made her feel stupid. She stood up and went to the mirror, looking at herself like she wasn't good enough for the first time in her life. She had never felt that way before. She used to think her caramel skin color was the shit, but now she wasn't too sure. Shit, her caramel skin couldn't pull the nigga she wanted so maybe she wasn't all that she thought she was.

She shook her head, knowing that she probably looked like a psychopath, and took a seat. She had wanted Biz to be for her and it was clear that he wasn't. The one man who was for her was dead. She looked at the time noticing that it was time for her to pick up her baby girl, Bee, from gymnastics class. She threw her hair up in a ponytail and snatched up her purse and phone and headed out the door. Just as she had gotten into her car, her phone began to ring.

She looked at the name seeing it was Bee's godfather then smiled.

West had been very active in Bee's life since she was born. After Benny had gotten killed, he had slowed down coming around but Missy didn't question it. West still made sure to make phone calls to check on how she and Bee were doing. Although she had been living paycheck to paycheck, she never let him know that. After Benny had died she would rather work for her money than to just be given anything. Everything came with a price and it had just so happened that the money Benny was splurging on her and their child came with a price as well. Except it was a price that Missy wasn't ready to pay for. Money was the root to all evil and she was almost a hundred percent sure that whoever had killed Benny, it was over money. It had been the most tragic day of her life and she didn't want to relive it. She couldn't take any more losses. Losing Benny had been the biggest one.

"Hey West, what's up," she answered.

"Ain't shit sis, just checking on you and lil' Bee," West responded. "How's work?"

"Work is good actually; I got a better job as a nanny. Thank God it's a black family," she lied partially while laughing. She was unsure if she still had her job but she knew if West knew that he would be bringing his dirty money to her.

"I know that's right. I'mma be in town soon, we should grab lunch or something or you can slap some shit on a grill," he replied chuckling. Missy shook her head as if West could see her, while chuckling.

"You and this grilled food, you ain't changed a bit."

"You damn right I didn't. So what's the word, you got me?" he asked.

"Of course," Missy replied, actually looking forward to a friendly face. She had grown so accustomed to being alone that she had forgotten that she had friends, although they never did come around a lot. West was different, he was family. After Benny died she had shut everyone out. Now that she was slightly feeling like herself, she was open to seeing old friends again.

CHAPTER 11

CHANGE

"Don't let a little dispute injure a great relationship."

— DALAI LAMA

Bonnie laid back in her bed as she rolled her eyes to the top of her head as Doc examined her. He had run what she felt like was a million different tests on her to make sure she was straight. She had been awake for two days and was ready to get back into the swing of things. She felt like she had already missed out on so much and now here Doc was still holding her back by not clearing her. "Doc, am I fucking cleared?" she asked, frustrated.

He shook his head from side to side. "Come on B, you know a nigga ain't gon' clear you if you ain't one hunned," Doc explained reasonably.

"Whatever," she replied, closing her eyes thinking about how much time had gone by. The only thing on her mind was catching up. She was still in shock that she had delivered twins, and her heart was feeling bigger and fuller. As Doc began to wrap everything up, the room door began to open slowly. Bonnie knew it was Biz in the room without even opening her eyes or saying a word. She felt his presence when he was around. It was something she had learned to do when she was in a coma. Her emotions were all over the place and she didn't want to show it. She wanted to remain the tough bitch she had always been, but somewhere deep down inside, she knew that would change. It seemed like everything around her was changing. She sat up in the bed once she heard Doc walk out the room leaving her and Biz inside.

"How you feeling ma?" he asked with his back against the wall and his hands in the pockets of his slacks.

"It doesn't matter, still not cleared," she responded while looking him dead in the eye. She still wasn't letting go of the fact that the first thing she saw when she had awakened was her man with his lips on another woman. Biz knew they would have to talk about it but Bonnie had been avoiding having that talk. Instead, she had been trying to learn their children and Biz saluted her for that. He knew she was uneasy about Missy, but he was here to reassure her that she had nothing to worry about. "Did you fuck her?" Bonnie asked while glaring at him in his eyes. She wanted to believe that he wouldn't lie to her in her face, that he wasn't that type of guy but truth be told, she didn't know him as well as she thought she did. She never would've thought that he would be intimate with another woman while she was incapable of doing so, and not because she was dead or anything but because she was comatose.

He shook his head from side to side while looking directly in her eyes. "Nah, a nigga ain't checking for her like that. And I wanna apologize for what you saw."

Bonnie wanted to call him a liar in every language she knew but awkwardly, she believed him. That was all the reassurance she needed but she wanted to put him to the test. "Fire her."

Biz knew that was coming and he shook his head from side to side once again, knowing that this time Bonnie wasn't going to be so kind. "You have nothing to worry about B. She convenient right now for the kids, she got them on a schedule. They are familiar with her and plus, you still ain't cleared. I've made it clear to her that another incident like that and she gon' have to bounce, don't worry ma. I handled it," Biz explained.

She rolled her eyes to the ceiling and scoffed, turning into the Bonnie he once knew. "That bitch got one time to cross the line and I'mma circle her ass in chalk. She needs to not let the dick get her fucked up. And since you captain save-a-hoe, if she fucks with me that's your ass," Bonnie said while getting up off the bed and walking out the room. Just as she reached the door, Biz grabbed her arm and pulled her into his chest.

"I missed the shit out you ma."

"Yea, yea, miss me with it nigga. Looked like you were getting real cozy with the replacement when I wasn't around," she replied smartly while pulling away from him and walking out the room.

As she entered the kitchen to find herself something to cook, she couldn't help but notice how much her children adored Missy. Their little laughs brought a smile to her face, but a feeling of guilt plagued her. Missy knew her children more than she did, and it was eating at her. Just as she was about to put herself a sandwich together, Cassidy's cry came through the air and Bonnie rushed out the kitchen and into the living room almost running to pick up her son.

"Aww, stink, what's the matter?" Bonnie cooed as she picked him up and bounced around trying to get him to stop, but the cries continued. She put her hands on his diaper to check if it was full and it wasn't. "You hungry papa?" she asked as she rocked back and forth.

Missy sat watching and she wanted to let Bonnie figure it out because she didn't want to overstep her boundaries, but the crying was driving her crazy. "He's due for a nap, do you mind if I take him?" she asked Bonnie.

Bonnie looked at her like she had three heads before responding.

"Actually, I do mind. I'm his mother and I need to get the hang of things. Thanks for the heads up tho." She sneered as she began walking up the stairs with her wailing baby.

Missy just shook her head from side to side, knowing that she had fucked up big time. There was no way she and Bonnie would get along. Although she was capable of being professional, Bonnie made it seem like they couldn't both co-exist in the same household. Missy had tried putting herself in Bonnie's shoes and she couldn't blame her. She would've probably been the same way if Biz was her man. Everything in her was telling her to quit, but she needed the extra money. Biz was paying her so well that she had quit her job at the supermarket, and she was able to live like she had been living. She was able to afford the luxuries that she'd once had when her husband was alive. Her daughter was able to live the life she was used to as well. Going back to living paycheck to paycheck wasn't even an option. She figured if they didn't fire her, she would stick around as long as she could. The best way to do that was to stay out of Bonnie's way.

"What's on your mind?" Biz asked as he entered the living room. He knew it had something to do with Bonnie.

"Nothing, feeling like I just don't belong here, but I need this job."

"B is very rough around the edges, but you do belong. The kids love you and you do a damn good job at what you do. I've talked to her, so we straight. Just give her space," Biz advised.

Missy nodded her head as she passed a yawning Cassie to him. "She needs a nap. While they are napping I'll run and get some groceries," she replied, trying to limit her interaction with Biz as well. She figured that that would probably help for Bonnie to take her hawk eyes off of her. She had gotten comfortable and slipped up, but she couldn't let it happen again. She was there to work and just wanted every conversation with Biz to be work related.

Biz noticed the change in her and he knew it was for the best. He watched as she walked out the door and headed up the stairs with

Cassie in tow. When he stepped into the nursery he noticed Bonnie sitting in the rocking chair with Cassidy laying on her chest drifting off to sleep as she sang him lullabies. He laid Cassie in her crib and she almost instantly went to sleep.

"I've missed out on so much. Look how big they are," she said with her voice cracking. She was beginning to get emotional. Biz stood behind the rocking chair putting his hands on her shoulders and massaging.

"You missed out on a little. They only four months, they got a lifetime with you ma," he reassured. He knew that the time that had gone by bothered Bonnie, but that was of neither of their control. It was inevitable and something they had to deal with and move on from. "He's gon' be a mama's boy," Bonnie said while looking down onto Cassidy's face and seeing him smile in his sleep as well as drool all over her chest.

"Miss me with that, don't be having him on no sucker shit," Biz joked.

"I still can't believe we got two little people," she said with a smile. Never in a million years did she even think about getting pregnant and having a child, let alone twins. In her twins she saw herself and Havoc. She knew that she had to raise her kids the right way because she didn't want them to go through what she and Havoc had. Shit, they were both fucked up in the head. She just wanted her kids to be the better version of her and her brother.

"Well believe it. I been staring at them for the past four months. They here to stay B."

"What's the word on Hav?" she asked as the thought of her twin brother crossed her mind.

"You know that nigga better than anyone out here. He searching high, he searching low, that nigga searching for us everywhere. I been busy here at the crib with you and the kids, so I ain't even had time to handle that. But soon as you good I'mma do him."

"Biz, let me handle him. He's my brother. Yea he done did some fucked up shit, but let me try to talk to him," Bonnie replied, almost pleading because she knew Biz's mind was already set.

"Talk to him? Ain't no talking to that nigga B, and you know it. I'd be damned if I lose you again to that fucking bird brain ass nigga," Biz hissed at her, careful not to wake his kids up. He walked out the room not wanting to even discuss the topic with her any further. His mind was set and that was it. But Bonnie wasn't letting it go that easily. She stood up and laid Cassidy in his crib and trotted out behind Biz.

She waited until they both got into the bedroom and she closed the door behind her, not wanting Missy to hear what was going on. "He won't hurt me. I know this because I can't hurt him. We been together from birth. What I can do is try to talk him out of coming after you."

Biz had already checked out of the conversation and it wasn't a debate. "Listen B, I told you what it is. Shit is nonnegotiable. We got kids now and that's who we need to live for. If this was a regular nigga in the street, I would okay you 'cause you would handle yourself accordingly. But this ain't. This a nigga who got the same skills that we got. Bottom line is I taught y'all everything y'all know. Not everything I know. I been letting it slide giving you some time but times up ma. He got to go."

Bonnie didn't even bother saying another word to him. Biz had made it nice and clear for her and although she didn't agree with him, she knew he was right. No amount of talking would stop Havoc, but also killing him wouldn't make her feel any better. She had to think of something, and fast.

CHAPTER 12

MEMORY LANE

"Memories warm you up on the inside, but they also tear you apart."

— HARUKI MARAKAMI

Ivory sat outside of the last place he remembered as home, looking at the house that had been newly remodeled. Although both of his parents had been murdered here, being here felt like home to him. This was his first time back since that tragic day and he never imagined that it would look the same. After all, it had been lit on fire. All the best memories in his life had happened in this home. He wondered if the inside looked the same. He had done his research on it to find out that it had been bought once and rented out a few times but never for too long. He knew why. Most people didn't want to live anywhere that people had died inside of. He was almost sure that the kids in the neighborhood would call it a haunted house if they knew the story behind it. But Ivory, he didn't see this home as that. He saw it as his family home. His mother and father's house to be exact. The for sale sign grabbed his attention and a smile came across his face. He had been saving up every penny he could get so he could buy his family house back. Every hit he did he had been motivated. All the money that Havoc had given him throughout the years he had managed to maintain but also save. It was all for this moment right here. He walked up to the door, knowing the owner was inside, with two briefcases full of money. He was determined to get back what was his and it would happen one way or another.

As he placed one of the briefcases down onto the floor, he used that hand to ring the bell. Almost instantly a woman opened the door and a slight frown fell upon her face as she noticed the kid that stood before her. She knew he wasn't over 18 and that he couldn't have been there to view the house. "I'm sorry sweetheart, I'm not interested in anything you are selling," she said as she tried closing the door on him. Ivory stuck his well-shined dress shoe in the doorway stopping her.

"I am not selling anything, I am here to buy," he replied, picking up his suitcase while pushing the door open farther so that he could enter the home. As he stepped in, all kinds of memories ran through his mind. In every room he had a memory and the nostalgic feeling began to take over him as he stood in awe. The woman looked on in confusion and proceeded to speak.

"How old are you?" she asked while sizing him up. Ivory had prepared himself for this moment. He knew he wouldn't be leaving this place until his name was on the deed.

"Eighteen," he replied, not giving her any eye contact but looking around his old home while digging in his suit pocket for his fake ID. He had learned that money made the world go round and with the right amount, you could make just about anything possible. The woman looked at the ID somewhat skeptical, but it seemed to check out. Nothing about it screamed forged but she continued on. After all, she hadn't had a viewing on the home in three months and was ready to get it off her hands. If this little boy wanted the problems the home came with, then he could have it.

"Okay, Mr. Sims, since you are the only viewing I have for the day, let's get this tour started," she stated as she began to direct him into the living room. "Over here we have a massive sitting room, perfect size for family functions. The fireplace has just been put in and so have these hardwood floors," she explained, but Ivory didn't pay her any mind. It was as if the house had transformed and he was looking at the living room the way his mother had perfectly decorated it. Images of his mother doing his hair that night popped into his head and his emotions began to run wild. He kept them in check, because he needed to close the deal.

He followed the lady into the kitchen where the island that his mother once had installed there was gone and instead replaced with a huge pantry. He made a mental note of getting it back once he sealed the deal. "Over here we have this country styled kitchen with a baker's oven and connection to this beautiful patio and an amazing view of the backyard. The floors have also been renovated in here along with this brand-new stove that has been installed," she spoke, but Ivory was no longer paying her any mind as his childhood began to come back to him once again. He looked out the window that sat above the kitchen sink but gave a view of the backyard, and he smiled. It had been many times that his mother had watched him from that exact window. He had played basketball in this same backyard and looked into the window to see his parents kissing and thought it was just disgusting. Right now as he stood there, he would give everything he had to get that back but he knew it was impossible. This feeling within him was what he missed. He had been taken in by Havoc and shown how to live his life. But there had always been a void and right now it was full. "I'll take it," was all he said as he stared at the woman. She hadn't even finished the tour of the house.

"Over here we have—" she tried to continue but once again, Ivory cut her off.

He opened up both briefcases revealing the neatly stacked money in them and responded again. "I said I will take it." That was all that she needed to see as a wide McDonald's smile came across her face. In her mind all she could think was 'good riddance' but in Ivory's mind, he couldn't help but to get her out of his hairs and be able to let his guard down and look at the other parts of his home and relish in the memories alone. Ivory couldn't be any happier to be in the only place he called home. This meant so much to him. He was home but being home also meant that he was one step closer to finding out the mystery behind who killed his parents.

They handled the paperwork and signed off, making sure to make everything look legit. In exactly two hours, young Ivory was now a homeowner. "It was great doing business with you!" the woman spoke up as she grabbed both briefcases, feeling like she had gotten over on Ivory, but that wasn't the case. He had actually shown her less money than he had intended on paying but she had taken the bait and ran with it. He shrugged his shoulders and walked her to the door with a smile just as big as hers on his face. "Same here. Have a good night," he replied while closing and locking the door behind her.

The minute the previous owner walked out, Ivory snatched his tie off his neck feeling like he was suffocating and tossed his suit jacket off onto the floor as he took another look around. All kinds of emotions ran through him but the very first one that surfaced was sadness. And for the first time in a long time, he cried his eyes out like never before. The years of tears he had built up all began to come raining down on his pants suit. This was a milestone for him, and although he cried tears of sadness, somewhere within a few of the tears was happiness. The guard he always had up was finally down and if felt good. If he remembered correctly, the last time he had actually cried was in this same home the night his parents were killed. Because from that moment, his childhood had been taken from him and he had to be the man that his father had been coaching him to be. And although he was young when his parents were taken from him, he never remembered seeing his father cry other than when his mother died. That had been the one exception. He walked up the stairs to his old bedroom where the events had taken place and it was as if it had just happened yesterday as the events played in his head. He had replayed in his mind multiple times the image of his mother and father's deaths. But standing there in his old bedroom, it all felt more real, like it had just happened. Ivory shook his head from side to side as he thought of how he could do nothing to save them. How his mother had lost her life actually trying to save him and his father trying to save her. It was like their deaths were domino effects. He walked out the room needing to catch a breath. Being in there he felt like a helpless kid again.

Ivory laid in the middle of the floor as his second emotion surfaced; he knew his mother and father would be proud of him. And although he hadn't turned out the way they had hoped, being able to purchase this home let him know that he was doing alright for himself in life. After all, how many boys his age were able to close a deal on a house in their name with their own money? Ivory was feeling like the man. He had purchased the house to finally have a home but to also relive the events of that night, hoping to find out who killed his parents. He wanted to deliver that person the same fate that they had mercilessly delivered his mother and father. Even after hearing the pleas, they didn't even have the decency to shield his eyes. He'd wanted to kill that person since the day he had left home. And meeting Havoc, he had prepared him for the task. He was going to make his parents' killer suffer the way they made him suffer watching both his parents die. Yea, they had let him go. But that was the biggest mistake that they had made yet. In fact, it was a mistake that he wouldn't make. Havoc had taught him the no witnesses rule and Ivory had stood by it, knowing that he had once been a witness to one of the worst crimes in his life and because someone had made a mistake leaving him as a witness, they were going to lose their life.

For the first time in a long time, Ivory felt at peace. This was his safe haven and he was determined to keep it a secret. He was sure he didn't know everything about Havoc and liked the idea of Havoc not knowing everything about him. At least that was what he thought. In fact, Havoc knew him a lot more than he had let Ivory know. He had saved Ivory's life that night, but he also knew that in that same instance he had taken Ivory's life, leaving him as a motherless and fatherless child. Ivory had been his good deed when he let him go. But no good deed goes unpunished and Havoc was going to learn that sooner than later.

CHAPTER 13

FAMILY FEUD

"Nobody wins when the family feuds."

— HOV

Bonnie sat in one of the tinted, untraceable cars that Biz owned in an oversized hoodie, sunglasses that covered the majority of her face, and a pair of black leggings. She had been staring at Havoc's house for the past fifteen minutes. She had managed to leave the house while Biz was consumed in his intense workout. It was the workout that he did before he was about to go out for a hit. She had unsuccessfully tried talking to him about squashing his and Havoc's beef, but Biz wasn't having it. Deep down, Bonnie knew that in a war between her man and her brother, her brother would lose. She couldn't stop two grown men from going at each other's throats, but it was worth a try. She had tried with Biz and been unsuccessful, and now it was time to try with her brother. She took a deep breath before tucking her mini Glock in her Ugg boot and putting one in her waist band as well as her hoodie pocket. She wasn't coming there for a war but if it came down to it, it would be a war that she didn't lose.

She exited the car and began jogging towards his front door. Just as she was about to knock, she changed her mind. Catching him off guard would be what was best in this situation. She headed to his backyard, jumping over his fence and straight to his back door.

Just as she had thought, the back door was unlocked. It had become a bad habit that Havoc had grown accustomed to after learning how to kill. He didn't think anyone would cross him trespassing his property 'cause if they did, he would put them in a grave and so far, no one had tried breaking in. Bonnie was the first. She entered his house and went directly into the living room where she saw him doing one-handed pushups.

"Look what the cat done drug in, what happened? You get tired of the nigga and kill him?" Havoc asked without pausing his workout. He had spotted Bonnie's car five minutes ago and was just wondering when she would make her move.

"Nah, in fact I came here to tell you to dead it. This beef shit is wack and draining. Plus, now you have a niece and nephew and I would like for you to see them," Bonnie replied, hoping that the mentioning of kids would butter him up. She knew about Havoc's soft spot for kids and was hoping that with Biz being his niece and nephew's father, he would stop the animosity.

Havoc stopped his workout and stood to his feet while glaring at her. "Since when you became the peacemaker type B? When you ever known to squash shit!? Just 'cause a nigga got you dick whipped don't mean nothing. He and I got some shit to settle and on god, I ain't gon' stop till it's settled."

Bonnie took a deep breath knowing that it was gonna be hard to get Havoc to let his and Biz's beef go, but she knew it wasn't impossible. "So just fuck ya niece and nephew, huh? You willing to try and put they father in the dirt and still think you gon' be around? I think the fuck not. In fact, nigga the person you should be mad at over Khalil's death should be Harper! Thanks to me, I killed that bitch while you were fucking her!"

Although she wanted to talk Havoc out of a war, her patience was beginning to run thin. It had been over two years and he was still after Biz; she was over the shit. After all, she had already taken care of the problem so she couldn't understand what his vendetta against Biz was really about.

"Oh, now you care about kids. Why, 'cause they yours? 'Cause as far as I remember your muzzle don't hesitate for anybody. What, you forgot?" Havoc replied, challenging her.

"Nah, I ain't forget shit nigga. You right, my muzzle and trigger finger take out anyone that's expendable. Including you. Let's call a spade a spade though. 'Cause ain't no way in hell Khalil's death got you this fucking hellbent. So, what's really up?"

"You know what's up! The nigga ain't loyal, that's what. Your ass tries to overlook that shit, but I can't. He killed K, and if it came down to it, he would kill you too! You forgot!? That the difference between you and I. I'mma go hard for mine when it's time. But like you said, everyone is expendable. You sound just like that nigga."

Bonnie shrugged her shoulders, unfazed and unmoved by her brother. "I go hard for mine; I can show you better than I can tell you Rashad. The ball is in your court twin. Don't start no shit you can't finish," she said before walking out his front door.

Havoc knew that Bonnie meant just what she had said. Without saying it verbatim, she had just told him that in a war between him and Biz, she was siding with Biz. He couldn't believe her. A war with his sister was never what he had intended. But if she couldn't let men play and overstepped her boundaries, a bullet had no name and he wouldn't try to save her. It was clear that she didn't want to be saved. She had picked a side and with the way she spoke, she was sticking with it.

* * *

Bonnie walked into the house and already, Biz knew where she had just come from. He gave her a piercing look, but she just ignored him. It didn't do her any better that he and Missy were both in the kitchen. Her mind was heavy and right now she didn't want to deal with either one of them. She walked straight into the living room where she could hear the twins. She stood with her back against the wall as she began watching them interact with one another, playfully laughing in their playpen. She couldn't get enough of them. Although she hadn't been cleared, she was happy to witness moments between them knowing that she probably had already missed out on so many. She just couldn't help but to wish that their bond remained the same forever. It was a bond that she had once shared with her brother that she never thought would break, but it was clear that after today, that was it. She couldn't understand why Havoc just wouldn't listen to her, but what she didn't know was that they were both alike. Both of them just wanted the other to see what they saw.

"Let me talk to you," Biz said in her ear as he walked by and began to ascend the stairs. Bonnie had thought about ignoring him, but instead she followed. She knew he had a bone to pick with her and in fact, she had a bone to pick with him as well. She couldn't understand why every time she walked into a room, he and Missy were together. She had believed him when he told her nothing went on between the two of them, but she couldn't help but to feel like something was still going on. She stepped in the room behind him and before he could talk she took the stand.

"Why is it that every time I come around, the two of y'all are akee keeing like y'all have known each other for years or some shit?"

"You ain't never heard of common courtesy? How to be kind? What, you ain't never joked with a nigga before? I need to teach you what it is?" Biz asked calmly and sarcastically with his eyebrows raised.

"You've taught me enough big fella. You also taught me that when my trigger finger is itching to handle it," she sneered.

"Go on now, kill the nanny if you want B," he replied while shrugging his shoulders and taking a seat on the bed.

His response was music to Bonnie's ears. "I thought you would never ask," she said as she took her hand out her pocket with her Glock that she had been palming since being at Havoc's house. She was ready to put someone to rest, anyone to rest, and Missy wasn't a bad contestant.

Biz jumped up from the bed and rushed over to Bonnie before she could fully make it out the room. He grabbed her arm and snatched her back in, slamming the bedroom door shut and pinning her against the wall. He shook his head as he reached for her gun, taking it out her hand and tossing it across the room. "You just always gotta be so crazy huh?" He chuckled. He wanted to be stern with her but instead, he was turned on by her. She had called his bluff and he was amused.

"You ever known me not to be?"

"Nah, but I know you crazy when I tell you not to do something, like go to Havoc's house, and you still do it."

Bonnie looked Biz in his eyes and stared for a few seconds before responding. "That's my brother, my flesh and blood. The same way Cassie and Cassidy are, that's how we once were. YOU came in between that. Are you fully to blame for our fallout? Probably not, but that's not important. The only thing you should be worried about is the fact that I chose you. Over my flesh and blood, I chose a man."

"Nah B, you chose your man," Biz said before giving her a kiss on her lips and kneeling down on one knee. He opened up the small ring box in his hand showing her the diamond encrusted Bezel-set that he had picked out for her. Bonnie nodded her head up and down, accepting the ring as Biz slid it on her finger. It wasn't the ideal proposal, but to her it was. She would've never thought Biz would settle down, nevertheless settle down with her. After he slid the ring on her finger his hands began to roam on her legs and up to her backside as he stood back up on his feet. Feeling another Glock behind her, he shook his head and she began to laugh. "Glad to know that you went there prepared," he said as he took the gun out her waistband.

Bonnie gave him a peck on the lips. "Stay ready ain't gotta get ready, right?" she said as she leaned into her boots pulling out another gun. Biz chuckled, and his dick jumped all at the same time. Bonnie wasn't your average woman, and he liked it. She was unpredictable and that was what made her all the more fun. As she sat her gun down onto the table, she walked over to him wrapping her long legs around his waist while he walked towards the bed.

He laid her on her back and helped her out of her leggings, putting her blossomed flower in his face. It had been so long and although she wasn't cleared, a little oral appreciation wouldn't hurt. He slowly licked from the entrance of her vagina to her clit, like a cat licking its fur. Bonnie shuddered at his touch. It felt like it had been decades since she had last gotten any action and just from his simple touch, she wanted to explode. But she wanted the feeling to last forever. She wrapped her legs around his neck as he began to pick up the pace while also slipping his finger in her tight walls. Although it was only his fingers, it caused her back to arch and a small moan to escape. "Oh my god daddy," she whined as the pleasure began to take over her body. Her fingers became entangled in his dreads and she began to pull on them, only making him go faster. He stuck another finger in her ass and instantly her body began to shudder. "OH SHIT!!!!" she screamed as the orgasm she had no control over left her body. It felt as if her soul was leaving and she couldn't help but to scream as she released herself.

Biz licked up every drop of magic that left her body and then some. Bonnie slid from under him snatching off her shirt and bra and went straight to his shaft. She didn't know it, but the touch of her fingernails against him made him want to bust a nut; instead, he let her get down on her knees and pleasure him. She sucked on his dick while wrapping both hands around it going up and down. This time it was Biz's turn to put his hand in her hair and grab with force. That only turned Bonnie on as she continuously moved her hand up and down while her mouth alternated from his dick to his balls. "Damn B!" Biz loudly whispered while his toes began to curl up. He couldn't hold back any longer. "I'm boutta nut ma."

That was all she needed to hear as she went faster and sucked harder. Cum shot in her mouth and she swallowed then pulled back, rubbing his dick and kids all over her chest. When he was done, they both laid back on the bed breathing heavily. Biz rolled over and kissed her on her forehead while getting up to clean himself up and get a rag. "A nigga gotta go to work ma."

Bonnie knew he was talking about the hit he had been preparing for, and she couldn't wait until she was back in tip top shape to do so as well. She had been under intense pressure and putting someone to sleep would definitely help.

CHAPTER 14

DADDY'S HOME

"Unraveling external selves and coming home to our real identity is the true meaning of soul work."

— SUE MONK KIDD

"Tag, you're it!" Beatrice yelled as she and her friends ran around her backyard. Missy stood in front of her grill, grilling up some shish kebabs, steak, hamburgers and chicken. It was a hot Sunday afternoon in Georgia and the perfect weather to be grilling. She was off and had invited over Bee's gymnastic friends as well as their parents to enjoy the weather with them. She had also invited Biz and West; it was the first time in a long time that she had invited anyone over. Ahead of time, Biz had already told her he couldn't be in attendance, but she had already known beforehand and just figured it was worth a try. She had been down about it for a second but figured that maybe it was also for the best. She hadn't made the best impression on his fiancée and to be quite frank, she didn't really want to hang with her. She had spotted the ring on Bonnie's hand the minute she saw her, and jealousy mixed with envy invaded her. It had been a week of wishing that ring was hers, but a girl could wish, right? Although Biz had never been hers the dream of him being hers was completely crushed with Bonnie in the picture. She tried not to dwell on it, and she didn't. There had been numerous times where Benny had told her "don't cry over spilled milk." And now was the best time to apply it to her situation.

She watched as her daughter and friends ran around the backyard enjoying themselves. It was a breath of fresh air for her. She just wished that smile that Bee wore could be permanent. But Missy knew there was nothing in this world that was. Just as she went to flip the burgers on the grill, she felt a pair of hands cover her eyes. "West, quit playing for you be the reason these kids eating charcoal for burgers," she joked.

West began to chuckle while removing his hands. "Nah, don't put that on me. I ain't tryna be chased down by a group of four and five-year-olds."

"UNCLE WEST!!!" Bee screamed, running full speed towards him and jumping in his arms.

"BB! What have you been eating girl? You weigh like a hundred pounds," he joked. Bee began to burst into laughter.

"No, I don't! You weigh like a hundred pounds."

"Girl, you wish," Missy chimed in causing West to nudge her shoulders as they both began laughing.

West put Bee back down onto the floor and kneeled down to her height. "BB go play; I have a surprise for you later," he whispered in her ear. Bee's eyes lit up like every other kid in the world when they heard the word surprise. She put her hand over her mouth and took off running to her friends bragging about her uncle having a surprise, although she had no idea what it was.

"Nigga, stop spoiling her rotten," Missy said rolling her eyes.

"Ah sis, it's okay, I got a surprise for you too." He chuckled. Missy just gave him a side-eye as she began taking the cooked foods off the grill.

"Help yourself. But before you do, please bring out the pan of baked mac and cheese, yams, and potato salad," she asked. West did a dramatic bow before responding.

"Anything for you, your highness."

Again, Missy rolled her eyes while chuckling. West and she had become good friends over the years, and his loyalty to Benny was unheard of. She knew he would catch a bullet for her family and that alone made him family. She began fixing Bee and her friends cheeseburgers while West came out with the main foods for the adults. "How's work sis?"

Missy smiled at the thought of Biz. "Work is good, and easy. And once again, they are black," she whispered to him, not wanting to offend the unseasoned meat at her house. West began to laugh while shaking his head. It was good to see Missy in good spirits. He hadn't seen her be her actual self in some time. "You forgot the potato salad. Want something done right, you gotta do it yourself," she added while walking back into her house.

"Bee, the burgers are ready!" she yelled as she entered the sliding doors.

When she entered the kitchen her heart dropped. It was as if she was staring at a ghost. It couldn't be. Standing there in the flesh was her husband Benny Lays. She wanted to jump, scream, shout, and cry but all in all, she was unable to do anything. Her knees began buckling as they became weak, and he reached for her. She backed away, unable to believe that he was really alive. She didn't want to be thought as crazy. For the first few months after his death she had felt like she was going crazy, hearing his voice and seeing his shadow. That was a place she didn't want to go back to. "No no no no, you're dead," she said shaking her head, trying to convince herself. But instead, he took another step towards her, this time touching her face.

"Nah ma, Daddy's home," Benny said, and that was when it all hit her. Tears began rushing out her eyes, and so many questions ran through her head.

"West said—"

"West said exactly what I told him to say," Benny cut her off.

She touched his face, his arms, and his chest, making sure she wasn't losing her mind. She laid her head on his chest so she could hear his heartbeat, and when she did, she still couldn't believe it. "How Benjamin, how?" she asked.

He led her out the kitchen and into their dining room and they both took a seat at the table before he decided to speak. Missy moved her chair away from him, still unable to understand. She saw he was alive but where had he gone, what took him so long to come back, why did he let her struggle, did he know how many nights she had stayed up crying over his death? So many questions infiltrated her mind and she wanted answers.

"How could you?" was the first question that was able to leave her lips as she glared at him.

"I had to ma, you know I would never intentionally leave you and Bee. That shit almost broke a nigga," he responded, trying to get her to understand. But it was clear her guards were up. He had expected this.

"So why did you do it and why are you back?" Missy interrogated.

"I did it because someone wanted me dead, and I'm back because you can help me."

Missy's eyebrows came together as she looked at him with a bit of confusion. "How can I help you Benny?"

"The person you work for tried to take me out. The name Biz ring any bells?" Benny asked.

Missy nodded her head with a shocked look on her face. "Biz did this?" she asked, unsure, and Benny nodded his head. Missy wanted to call him every liar known to man but she knew she couldn't. Although he had been gone, he hadn't been gone that long and she knew he would probably knock her out if she went against him. She had never heard Biz raise his voice, so to think that he tried to kill her husband bothered her. She did a good job not wearing her thoughts on her sleeve because Benny sat there trying to read her and was coming up short.

"Why?"

Instantly, rage took over Benny as he leaned forward in his seat and wrapped his hand around her neck and squeezed. "DOES IT FUCKING MATTER WHY?! THE NIGGA TRIED TO TAKE ME OUT IN FRONT OF MY FUCKING FAMILY!" he yelled.

Missy used her free hand to slap him causing him to loosen up off of her. She didn't believe Benny, not even a little bit and with the way he had just choked her, a little tighter and she would've been dead. She wasn't taking that chance.

"What do you want me to do?" she asked as she scowled.

"When the time is right, I will tell you. For now, keep going to work and keeping shit casual," Benny responded in the same menacing tone. Although she had questioned him, he knew Missy would fall through with the plan. All of this was just too much for her to take in. He couldn't understand why she wanted to know his business all of a sudden but pushed it to the back of his mind. Right now the only thing on his mind was seeing his daughter. "Go get Bee," he instructed while rubbing his beard.

Missy stood to her feet, trying to look as normal as possible. She walked into the kitchen and splashed water onto her face and dabbed with a paper towel. She didn't need any of these white folks in her business and right now she had toddlers and preschoolers to tend to. She took a deep breath before plastering on a fake smile while grabbing the potato salad and heading back out into the backyard.

She sat the potato salad on the table and looked over to West sending daggers his way. She was gonna deal with him later, but right now she wanted Bee to see her father as well. She knew her daughter would take better to the surprise than she did. "Bee, come with me inside really quick so we can change your shoes," she said, and Bee wore a pouty face as she walked towards her mother.

"But Mom." Missy shot her a look that made her stop right in her tracks. They walked into the house and Missy pulled out her phone to record.

"The shoes that I want you to wear are in the dining room," she instructed. Although Bee wasn't happy, she took off running because she wanted to get back outside with her friends. Missy stayed hot on her tail. When Bee reached the dining room her jaw dropped open as she looked at her father.

"I missed you baby girl," he said breaking the silence. Bee said nothing, instead she took off running and jumped into his arms as tears began to fall from her eyes. She was in complete, utter shock, and the moment alone made more tears well in Missy's eyes as she turned off her camera and walked over to Benny and Bee. He pulled her into their embrace and all that could be heard were the light cries from Bee and Missy. Bee had never though she would see her father again and Missy didn't know about the can of worms that had just been opened. She knew Benny enough to know that he wanted Biz dead and with the way her heart felt, she just hoped she could be of much use and deliver.

CHAPTER 15

MOMMY DEAREST

"When you look into your mother's eyes, you know that is the purest love you can find on this earth."

— MITCH ALBOM

"Hey, Is, I miss you!" Cyn spoke to her daughter through a facetime call. She had left her baby behind in Florida with her mother, the only support system that she had. She had come back to Georgia in hopes of seeing Biz again and approaching a situation that she had avoided for so long. After Biz had left, Cyn didn't even bother looking for him. She had told him once she wasn't going to force him to be a father and she meant it. In fact, she had been doing a damn good job raising Isabella by herself. It wasn't until recently that Isabella had begun asking questions about her father and Cyn felt that she deserved answers as well. It had taken her years to make the move to come back to Atlanta, but after a while she felt like she owed it to her daughter. After all, she didn't make Isabella by herself. Biz was her dad and Cyn wanted him to be held accountable for his actions. She stared at her daughter's mahogany skin and full eyebrows with her curly hair up in a ponytail and just smiled.

"I miss you too Mommy. Guess what?" Isabella responded.

"What baby?"

"Mommmm I'm not a baby, look!" Isabella said with a wide grin showcasing her missing tooth. Cyn put on the most shocked face, acting as if this wasn't the fifth tooth that Isabella had lost.

"Did the tooth fairy come?" Cyn asked.

Isabella gave her a frowned look before responding. "Come on Mommy, I know you and Grandma are the tooth fairy. I told you I'm not a baby."

Cyn nodded her head and shrugged her shoulders. Isabella was growing before her eyes. It had been a memorable eight years, in fact the best eight years she had in her life, and she couldn't believe that her baby girl was about to be nine. The sound of footsteps behind her made her hurry and get off the phone with her baby. She didn't know much about Biz, Benny and Havoc but she knew that she was dealing with some killers. As she turned around, she saw Havoc standing against the kitchen counter with an apple in his hand.

"That was ya lil' girl?" he asked while eyeing Cyn. Her hair fell over her shoulders and what she wore left little to imagination which made Havoc's dick hard. With a spaghetti strap camisole and undercut booty shorts on, he couldn't help himself. Cynthia was beautiful and there was no denying it. Cyn stood back staring at Havoc as she noticed his hard dick through his grey sweats. She was just as infatuated with him. Havoc had a boss stance about him; in fact it was that very same thing that had drawn her to Biz. She walked over to him stepping close enough for her nipples to rub on his chest as she grabbed a banana from behind him.

"Yep, and she isn't up for discussion," she stated while walking away and standing at the other end of the counter. Havoc put his hands up in surrender mode, understanding her. She didn't know him from a whole in the wall, and although he had allowed her to stay with him so he could keep a close watch on her, that meant nothing. They weren't on that page yet.

He watched as she peeled the banana and Cyn could feel his eyes on her. Being one to put on a show, she put the banana as far behind her throat as she could making the entire thing disappear. Havoc chuckled to himself while placing the apple down. He knew what kind of games Cyn was playing and he was about to show her he didn't play games. He walked over to her picking up her small body and placing her on the counter. His hand instantly began to roam as he ran his tongue across her neck causing her to moan. He pulled her shorts to the side and inserted two fingers into her warm box, penetrating slowly as her juices covered his fingers. She was like a waterfall; he had never felt someone so wet in his life. Cyn's back began to arch as small moans escaped her lips. She didn't know where the kids were and didn't want them to hear, but it was hard to not make noise. She used her feet to pull down his grey sweats and once they were successfully down, without hesitation, he removed his fingers while placing them in her mouth while slowly entering her. Cyn licked his fingers clean loving the way she tasted; nobody could tell her that she didn't taste like dark chocolate.

Havoc picked her up off the counter and pounded in and out of her, causing her to scratch his back and moan loudly. "Fuckkkkkk!"

Her moans fell on deaf ears as he continued to work his magic. Just as they were both reaching their climax, Cyn made sure to get off first before jumping out of Havoc's arms and getting straight on her knees sucking him. She had been wanting to taste him for a while but had been intimidated. Also, the fact that he was Vee's old fling left her feeling some kind of betrayal to her old friend. But she had just gotten caught up. Even a blind man could tell that Havoc was fine as hell. And after sucking his dick until his kids ran in her mouth, Cyn was here to tell the world that his dick game matched his looks.

She licked up every drop before standing on her two feet and getting herself together and walking out the kitchen as if it never even happened. Havoc flashed a small smile, liking how she wasn't asking for anything more. It was clear they were on the same page. They had both wanted sex and had gotten it and could go about their business.

He walked out the kitchen and headed to his bathroom to get himself washed up, but not before peeking into CJ's room and seeing him sitting there staring at a blank wall. Havoc was at the end of the road when it came to trying to parent CJ. He knew that he couldn't. In the blink of an eye CJ's life had changed. Havoc had tried giving him the normalcy that he needed but knew it wasn't doing the young boy any justice. He wanted to hold it down for Khalil and most of all Harper, but he couldn't. He wasn't made for this. The lifestyle he lived didn't allow him the fortune to become someone's parent. He didn't understand how Bonnie thought she could do it, but he knew in the long run it would bite her in the ass. Children were liabilities, and CJ had already been a liability once. Havoc knew that CJ deserved better but he was stuck on what to do with the young boy. He was already seeing a change in his behavior. CJ had begun killing animals for fun and Havoc knew it wasn't a good sign. He knew that the life that CJ was being exposed to was what made him begin acting the way he acted. It was as if killing had become normal all because he witnessed his mother's death. It didn't help that he didn't talk either. Havoc wanted to be there for CJ the best way he knew how but his best wasn't enough. Ivory had been the one helping CJ cope but in fact, Havoc hadn't seen Ivory in a few days. He put it in his mental note to call Ivory and make sure he was straight. He knew that if anyone could relate to CJ, it was Ivory. After all, he had also witnessed his parents being gunned down in cold blood. Maybe there was some way that he could help CJ get through it. Havoc shrugged his shoulders and shook his head, going into his bathroom thinking about what exactly it was he wanted for CJ. Yea he wanted to keep him around, but it was clear he wasn't doing a great job. The thought of giving CJ up to the system was the last thought that crossed his mind as he stepped into the shower to clear his mind.

CHAPTER 16

REGULAR PROGRAMMING

"Baby tell me why, why I got to try so hard. You got me craving your attention."

— EVAN ROSS

"You're cleared," Doc said as he put away his stethoscope. He looked at a grinning Bonnie and chuckled. He knew those words were like magic to her soul and with the look on her face, he knew he was right.

"You hear that Biz! IM CLEARED!!" she yelled as if they weren't in the same room. Her excitement caused him to chuckle at her as well. Seeing her this way, she resembled a kid. He walked over to Doc giving him a brotherly embrace.

"Thank you, man. I left something in ya trunk," he said, and Doc already knew what it was. Biz was generous with his money when it came to the little bit of friends he had. Doc had been loyal since day one, so dropping five mil in his trunk was nothing to him. Doc had earned every dollar, and because Biz couldn't thank him enough, he let his money do the talking.

Doc nodded his head before heading out the bedroom leaving the two lovebirds to enjoy one another. Bonnie walked over to Biz and wrapped her arm around his neck and ran her tongue across his earlobe. It had been a week since their oral fest, and now that she was cleared, she was ready to take him down. Biz's shoulders shuddered and he returned the favor by running his tongue across her earlobe and neck. A slight moan escaped Bonnie's lips and he began to smirk. He pulled away and walked towards his walk-in closet and Bonnie followed behind him confused and baffled.

"Unh uh, nigga. I been running around in heat for the longest and you are not about to turn me the fuck down. This pussy is wet, tight and ready," she fussed while her vagina throbbed at the mere sight of Biz. He gave a short laugh before stripping out of his house clothes and into work clothes.

"Relax B, a nigga gon' give you exactly what you want. But right now, we got a hit. Now you can come or get left, you pick," he replied. He knew there was no way Bonnie would stay home while he went on a hit. She had been out of commission for so long he knew her trigger finger was itching and ready to kill.

"Oh, should've started off with that, instead of getting a bitch ready to fuck. I thought you would never fucking ask," Bonnie replied, getting undressed beside him. She had missed having hits; she had missed her work clothes as well. She slipped on an all-black body suit with a pair of black thigh high boots, and pulled her hair out of the ponytail it was in and placed some lip-gloss on her lips. Biz couldn't help but to lick his lips at the sight of her. She had him questioning if he should dick her down right there in the closet before they went but knew he was on a time crunch.

"Come here," he instructed, and Bonnie did just as she was told. He slid back a small compartment that was built into the wall and placed his hand there while it scanned, confirming his identity. He began to push a few buttons then instructed Bonnie to put her hand there just as he had done. After the machine scanned her hand, he turned to her and smiled. "Now you have access to my life."

Before Bonnie could even ask what exactly it was that he meant by that, the entire wall slid to the side giving them access to an entirely new room. Filled with guns and ammo, Bonnie was in awe. Biz had every gun that had been made from the 80's to current. He flashed a smile at her as she looked around amazed. He felt like a proud dad showing off his trophies. Along another wall there were different swords of all different sizes and symbols.

"I didn't know you were a collector," Bonnie spoke, breaking the silence as she looked at all the swords he had gotten from different countries.

"There's a lot more you gon' learn about me ma," Biz said while walking over to a casing that held his smaller guns. Bonnie followed and they both filled their magazines and began tucking guns. While Bonnie kept it simple placing one in her boot and her bra, Biz placed one in his boot as well while placing two on his hip. "You can never be too careful ma."

Bonnie nodded her head in understanding and took a look around the room one more time before walking out. She couldn't believe that she had been here all this time and had no idea about the safe room. She smiled at how smooth Biz was. In fact, she was proud to call him her man.

She walked out the room and into the kitchen where Missy was making her kids a bottle and just stared at her, sizing her up. She didn't know what it was about Missy, but she rubbed her the wrong way. But because Biz had insisted on her staying, that was the only reason she was still around. Bonnie was just waiting on her to breathe on her too hard so she could be all up in her ass. She'd had it out for Missy since the first day she had awakened and until she was out of her hairs, she would continue to be a bitch. She didn't understand why Biz wanted her around and in fact, it was a topic that needed to be touched on. Yea the kids were familiar with her but with Bonnie now being cleared, she could take care of her own children.

She could tell that she made Missy uncomfortable, but did she care? No. She was the HBIC aka Head Bitch in Charge and wanted Missy to understand that at all times. She walked out the kitchen and into the living room where her babies were all smiles in their playpen. She had been trying to spend as much time with them as she could but it seemed like they were so fond of Missy, they didn't pay their actual mother any mind. Bonnie tried pushing the thought to the back of her mind but deep down inside, it hurt. It hurt to know that the two beautiful souls that came out of her stomach were attached to someone that wasn't her. She leaned over and picked up Cassidy flashing her a smile and giving her a kiss on the cheek. In those two seconds, Cassie went from a happy baby to a raging one. Bonnie frowned checking her diaper, and seeing she was clean. She couldn't understand why and wished that she could ask her baby and get an answer.

As Missy walked over to the playpen to pick up Cassidy with his bottle in her hand, Cassie began screaming even louder and reaching for her. Bonnie's tolerance level was at an all-time low when in reality, Missy hadn't done anything. She had done what every parent would've wanted their nanny to do, form a bond with their child. But Bonnie didn't see it that way. She saw it as Missy was trying to steal her man and steal her children.

Biz walked into the living room seeing a confused Bonnie. He knew she hadn't gotten all the ropes together with the children and they were still warming up to her. He knew she didn't understand, but he did. He walked over to her kissing her cheek and decided to help her out a bit. He stuck his face in Cassie's causing her face to dry up like the Sahara Desert. He played, he pouted, he tickled her, all making her and Bonnie's day better. Seeing a smile on the both of their faces made him feel good. About five minutes later, the two were out of the door and on their way to end somebody's life.

CHAPTER 17

THE TRUTH

"I've made up my mind, don't need to think it over. If I am wrong, I am right, don't need to look no further."

— ADELE

"Oh, now you care about kids. Why, 'cause they yours? 'Cause as far as I remember your muzzle don't hesitate for anybody. What, you forgot?... Nah, I ain't forget shit nigga. You right, my muzzle and trigger finger take out anyone that's expendable. Including you."

The sound of Bonnie's voice continued to play in Ivory's head. He knew her voice from anywhere. That voice had made him shiver for many nights as a child and made him have several nightmares, which had resulted in him peeing in the bed and getting whooped with an extension cord by his foster mother. He had overhead Havoc and Bonnie's conversation a week ago and it was weighing heavily on his shoulders. All types of emotions and questions ran through his mind. He sat in his old bedroom with his knees to his chest, as the memories came flooding back to him.

"I love a little game of Russian roulette, don't you? Come on." Ivory shook his head, wanting to get her tormenting voice out of his head. The realization of Bonnie's voice made him shake his head in denial. Bonnie had never pulled the trigger successfully. She had tormented him and his parents, but that was all. Her partner was the one who had pulled the trigger killing both his parents in cold blood without a wink. Ivory had put two and two together and instantly his heart began to race. Tears began to form in his eyes as he felt the sting of betrayal. He didn't want to believe that Havoc was the one who killed his parents. He had spent too many nights thanking God for bringing Havoc into his life. And now years later, he was realizing that Havoc had been the reason that his life had been turned upside down in the first place. If Havoc would've never killed his parents, he would've never needed him as a mentor to begin with. The thought of Havoc knowing all along made him sick to his stomach. He hadn't said a word or even acted like he knew Ivory, but he was no longer the dummy in this situation. Ivory knew Havoc knew exactly who he was, and the only thing that made him take Ivory under his wing that day was the guilty conscience that he had. That same conscience that allowed him to let Ivory run.

Ivory wanted to confront him, but there was no way that Havoc would willingly tell him the information unless he was going to kill him. Havoc had allowed him to walk away free once, but he knew that once he told Havoc what he knew that would be the end of it. He would be reunited with his parents again.

The tears in Ivory's eyes began to fall as the frustration began to build. He felt deceived and belittled. Havoc had played him like a little kid, and now he felt more stupid than ever. He had held Havoc on a pedestal so high that not even he could reach it. He thought of Havoc just as highly as he thought of his own father and wished that he didn't, only because it was an insult to his dad. He had been willing to lay down and die for Havoc feeling a sense of loyalty to him. And now he realized that in fact, it should've been vice versa. Havoc had played him, not the other way around. The thought of him doing the unthinkable bothered Ivory but he knew he had opened Pandora's box with his revelation. He had vowed every day since he was a kid that when he found out who killed his parents, he would kill them. And now that he had found out, he was unsure of how to deal with the news. Havoc had to get handled one way or another. But the thought alone of crossing the one man who taught him everything he knew haunted him. Havoc had fucked up ultimately, but he had given Ivory a better life. Ivory tried to weigh the situation out seeing if the good outweighed the bad, but in reality, if Havoc hadn't done bad in the first place, there would be nothing to outweigh. He closed his eyes and went back to the moment that Havoc had let him go. He couldn't understand why he hadn't known sooner. He looked Havoc in those same eyes on a daily basis and hadn't known. He had been blinded by the kindness that Havoc had shown him. Although he may have been blinded, knowing that Havoc had known all along, he didn't know how that made him feel. He had once felt like the son that Havoc didn't have but now, he felt like his puppet. He had done hits for Havoc and anything he asked because he wanted to prove himself. But why did he need to prove himself to a coward? Someone who shot a woman while her back was turned. Ivory just shook his head. He had heard so much about Bonnie and how ruthless she was from Havoc, almost making Ivory fear more than he knew he already did. But now he realized that Havoc was the more ruthless twin. How else could he have killed someone and taken their child under his wing? That was the most dangerous thing of all.

It had never even dawned on him that he had never met Bonnie, and now it all made sense. Bonnie thought he was dead, and Havoc had kept Ivory a secret from her. Ivory shook his head still in disbelief. Had Havoc accidentally found him that night he ran away from his foster mother's house? Or was this all part of his plan? Ivory had a million questions for his mentor, and he wanted answers, and was gonna make sure he got them. As his anxiety began to run wild, he stood to his feet and looked around his old bedroom one more time, reliving the night one last time. When he walked out the room he closed and locked the door, vowing that, that was the last time he would relive those moments. He had found out who pulled the trigger and until he ended Havoc, he didn't want to step foot back into that bedroom.

He walked downstairs and rolled himself a blunt while taking himself a seat on his couch. He had almost gotten the entire living room to look just how he remembered it. The only thing that was missing was the big family picture that sat on the wall; that was something he could never get back. So instead he left the wall blank and used his photographic memory of the family portrait every time he looked up. Tears began to cloud his vision just as his phone began to ring. He looked down and a flame lit up inside him. It was Havoc. He wanted to question him right then and there but decided against it. He knew it wasn't the right time. In fact, when he did question him about the situation he wanted to be able to look him in his eyes, those same eyes that had set him free. He thought about letting the phone ring until it went to voicemail but decided against it, not wanting to raise any red flags. He always answered Havoc's call and if he started not to now, then he was sure Havoc would know something was up.

He wiped away the tears and cleared his throat before speaking. "Yo."

"What's good Ivy, fuck you been at lil' nigga?" Havoc responded. It took everything in Ivory just to play it cool.

"Man, I been chilling, keeping my ears to the street. I left ya crib to give you and that new shorty some space," he lied in a joking tone. He had left because he couldn't stand the sight of him and couldn't trust himself around Havoc. Shit, it would be nothing for Havoc to finish the job once he felt the shift in Ivory's vibe.

Havoc began to chuckle. "You know that ain't necessary. Shit, CJ ass need someone to cope with. I was hoping you could swing by and get the lil' nigga, spend some time with him. Shit, I'm clueless when it comes to shit like this," he explained.

Ivory inhaled some smoke while nodding his head as if Havoc could see him. "Aight I'mma spin the block then pull up and get the lil' man."

"Good looking," Havoc thanked him.

Ivory hung up the phone, not wanting to talk any further than he had to. He really didn't know why he had agreed to get CJ but knew that in reality, he could do better for CJ than Havoc did. Havoc was a snake, and CJ didn't deserve him. He knew that Havoc would fuck CJ up the same way he did him. Even though he didn't want to admit it, but he knew Havoc was right, maybe he could help CJ out. They had more in common than they thought. Plus, Havoc wouldn't be around much longer, so he wanted to make sure CJ was comfortable with him. He wouldn't allow him to be put in the system how Havoc let him. The system would do nothing but destroy him, and CJ had been through enough. He was gonna be better than Havoc. Although he would take away CJ's guardian, he was sure he could be a better guardian to CJ than Havoc could ever be.

CHAPTER 18

'19 BONNIE AND CLYDE

"Mami's a rider and I'm a roller, put us together how they gon' stop both us."

— HOV

Biz sat at the craps table in the busy casino while keeping his eyes on the prize. His target Rio Cortez, head of the Dominican cartel, sat across from him. Biz had sat at this craps table for three weeks sizing up his target, unbeknownst to him. Biz had studied him long enough to know that he had four body guards. Two at the machines, one on the second floor, and one at the table. Rio kept a strict schedule where he attended the casino four out of seven days of the week. Once Biz had learned that, he too had begun coming more frequently. As Biz prepared to roll the dice, he looked up towards the balcony and gave a wink to Bonnie as she flashed him a smile. Right before he was about to roll the dice, his eyes were directed to the woman behind her, and it was as if his eyes were playing tricks on him, but they weren't. Standing there in the flesh was Cynthia. He hadn't seen her in years since he walked out on her. She hadn't aged a bit and in fact, her body was looking better than he remembered.

"Any day now," Rio said as he looked at Biz impatiently. Without looking, Biz rolled the dice, causing everyone at the table to erupt in a cheer. Biz looked down seeing that he rolled seven. He looked around the table and saw that instead of betting with him Rio had betted against him. He reached over the table and slid all of Rio's chips towards him.

"Deal me out," Biz said, knowing that in a minute Rio was about to do the same. Biz had learned that Rio refused to lose a certain amount of money and right now he was sure that he had exceeded his limit being out five hundred grand. He looked back up to the balcony and Cyn was no longer there. He diverted his eyes back to the table as they counted out his money. He watched as Bonnie headed towards the bathroom the minute Rio stood from the table. Biz too stood up and began to walk out the doors of the casino. He passed his ticket to valet and just as the man jogged off to get his car, Biz felt the butt of a gun crash down on the back of his head instantly knocking him out.

As Bonnie walked out the bathroom, she looked around the casino seeing that Rio and his men were gone, which meant Biz was gone. They had anticipated this very move and she had shaken her head at how predictable they had been. As she began to walk towards the exit, she felt the stare of someone across the room. Bonnie stopped in her tracks looking around to see where that energy was coming from and her eyes connected with Cyn. She made a mental note of her to be extra cautious, thinking that maybe she was one of Rio's people. She waved the girl off and walked out the casino just as valet was pulling up. She hopped in the car and drove in the parking lot and slowed down when her eyes set on Rio's SUV. She read the plate and a smile crept on her face. She wasn't late to the party; in fact, the party was just about to begin. Her adrenaline began rushing and excitement began to take over her. It had been so long since she had felt this rush and now it was back. She knew that this hit would release a lot of the built-up tension she was holding in and couldn't wait to get it all out. She drove carefully behind the car, leaving five cars in between them as she followed.

After about fifteen minutes, the black SUV came to a halt at a warehouse. Bonnie just sat back in the far distance, happy that the sun was going down so she could hardly be noticed. She leaned her seat back and watched as the two bodyguards in the back and Biz exited the truck. She waited until she saw Rio exit as well while instructing his other two bodyguards to stand watch. She looked at her watch and saw that she still had three minutes before she made her exit. Biz had been clear with his instruction and precise, and she was going to follow it to the T. While she waited, she screwed on her silencer before kissing it. She couldn't wait to pop off.

Just as the clock hit the exact minute, Bonnie looked outside her window and saw both security guards on their phones. She shook her head knowing that this was gonna be easy. She walked over to them with her heels clacking against the gravel, causing them both to look up and place their hands on their guns but once they saw that it was a woman, they both loosened up, putting their hands down. Bonnie gave them a small smile before speaking.

"I'm looking for my fiancé, he just came out of your car. You wouldn't have seen him, would you?" she asked while taking her gun out her boot and shooting a whole through the both of their heads. She shook her head and chuckled. "Mama still got it. Gotta be quicker than that," Bonnie whispered to herself. She took pride in knowing that her aim was lethal, and her speed was even quicker. She had managed to take both of them out in a split second, not even allowing them to fully touch their guns. She cracked the door of the warehouse open slowly and without hesitation, she took out the other two bodyguards. Her eyes were set on Biz who Rio had a gun to.

"Ah, ah, ah, I don't think you wanna do that Princessa," Rio said while shaking a finger for emphasis. He kept his gun trained on Biz and Bonnie kept hers trained on him. "You lift a finger, I blow his brains out. Now you wouldn't want that, would you?"

Bonnie shook her head from side to side making Rio feel like he was in command. "Put your gun down and I'll put mine down," she responded.

"Oh come on, Princessa. You think I was born yester—" POP

Bonnie shot a bullet clean through his head causing him to drop dead. She had learned earlier on in the game that conversation made gunmen vulnerable. They thought they were negotiating when in reality, it was stalling. She walked over to Biz and untied him from the chair he was sitting on.

"You did good ma."

"Of course, did you forget who I am?" she asked as she blew the muzzle of her gun before tucking it back in her boots. Biz followed her lead as they both walked out the warehouse without a single hair on their heads misplaced. They jumped in the car deciding to head home to their babies as Jay Z and Beyoncé played through their speakers singing their ghetto love song.

Cyn sat back in a car watching Bonnie and Biz drive off like the happiest couple in the world. Anger began to emanate through her with fear. She had just witnessed Bonnie commit a quintuple homicide. She didn't know what exactly it was she was dealing with when it came to Biz. It seemed like everyone associated with him killed for a living and she was unsure if she wanted to bring that into her daughter's life. She knew that Biz had already seen her and knew that it would only be some time before they had to meet. She hadn't told Havoc where she was going because he had made it clear that he wanted Biz dead. But first Cyn needed to speak to him and then Havoc could have his way with him. She needed Biz to know that their daughter had been asking for him and wanted to meet him. She wanted to turn away and go back to Florida, but she was in too deep now. She wanted to see what Biz was really about. They had always kept their private lives private, but it was clear that Biz was no Wall Street banker. She thought about tailing them but chose to go against it. She knew that if she had been made one more time by either Biz or Bonnie, she would be receiving a bullet hole just like the men she had just put out. Cyn shook her head and drove in the opposite direction, knowing that sooner than later she would face Biz. She just needed the timing to be right and then she would make her move.

CHAPTER 19

TRAP BOYS

"Say my lifestyle extravagant, I talk cash shit, bitches say I'm arrogant."

— GUCCI

Ivory sat on the balcony of one of the traps that his good friend Ezekiel aka Eazy ran. The two had become friends four years ago, both trying to find their footing in the world. While Ivory chose killing, Eazy chose trapping. The two led two completely different lives but made sure to maintain a friendship. Although Ivory was only fourteen and Eazy was eighteen, the age difference between the two meant nothing. Eazy was the big brother Ivory never had.

"Damn Ivory, you done licking and caressing the blunt yet?" Ezekiel's girlfriend Khloe joked.

He looked down at the blunt seeing it rolled to perfection and began to chuckle. His mind was still on Havoc. He knew what he had to do but, he felt like he needed a masterplan. Taking Havoc down wasn't just any ole regular hit. Havoc had taught him everything he knew and here he was thinking of a way to outsmart him.

Ezekiel also chuckled while looking at Ivory. He had noticed since the minute he pulled up to the trap door that his mind wasn't right, and if Khloe could see that something was on his mind, then it must've been serious. He nudged his head into Khloe's neck giving her a kiss and inhaling her scent. "Let me talk to my mans real quick," he whispered into her ear. She nodded her head and stood to her feet reentering the house, giving them space. As soon as she was out of earshot Ivory lit the blunt taking a long drag from it.

"Damn nigga, what happened, you got some broad knocked up? Or you caught the package?" Eazy joked. Ivory began to laugh causing the smoke in his lungs to burn as he began coughing. He shook his head passing the blunt as he tried to catch his breath.

"You a funny nigga," he responded once he got himself together.

"Nah, but deadass, what's up?" Ezekiel asked, seriously concerned, before he took a pull.

"Found out who killed my parents," Ivory said in a low tone while putting his head down like he was ashamed. Ezekiel pulled his gun out of his pocket and cocked it back placing it on his lap, ready to catch a body for his friend.

"Baby boy, what you waiting on? Why that nigga still got air in his lungs? Say the word and that nigga is dead."

A small smile came across Ivory's face. Eazy had always been a hundred with him and down for whatever. Although Ivory was younger, he was the more levelheaded out of the two. Eazy had been through just as much as Ivory and that was why they connected on the level they did. Both orphans that were thrown in the system and found their way out while fending for themselves. Ivory and Eazy had made it clear they were boys for life.

"Who killed them?"

"Havoc," Ivory responded while looking at his best friend. Ezekiel's face looked as if he had seen a ghost. He couldn't believe it. He had seen Havoc around a couple times, and Ivory had always spoken so highly of him it was unbelievable.

"I know you fucking lying," he said while looking at Ivory, to see if he was really serious. But the look on Ivory's face said it all. "Wait, you really deadass?"

Ivory nodded his head while looking Eazy in his eyes. Eazy just shook his head in disbelief. He knew that Ivory was crushed. And from the stories he had heard from Ivory, he knew that when it came to Havoc you had to come correct; there was no half stepping when it came to him. He put the blunt out deciding he needed a clear mind to process his thoughts. "So, what's the plan? You know there ain't no guns blazing when it come to that nigga."

Ivory nodded his head and shrugged his shoulders. "I haven't thought of a plan yet. When I do make my move I wanna make sure it's executed. I gotta plan this shit and keep my emotions under wraps," Ivory explained. Ezekiel nodded as well knowing that if anyone knew how to attack this situation it was Ivory, so he wouldn't input himself unless he was needed.

REAL ASS BITCH GIVE A FUCK 'BOUT A NIGGA, BIG BIRKIN BAG HOLD FIVE, SIX FIGURES! STRIPES ON MY ASS SO HE CALL THIS PUSSY TIGGER, FUCKING ON A SCAMMING ASS, RICH ASS NIGGA!

City Girls' "Act Up" began to blare through the speakers and Ivory looked up at Eazy who just chuckled and shook his head. "You know Khloe probably in there with her chicken head ass friends," he spoke while getting out his seat. Ivory followed him into the house and just as Eazy had said, Khloe and her chicken head ass friends were in the house and all of them were twerking all over the trap furniture. Ivory chuckled while shaking his head and scanning the room. His eyes instantly fell on the one girl who wasn't twerking and she piqued his interest. She was light brown with shoulder-length hair, and the only thing Ivory could stare at were the freckles that donned her cheek. He had never seen a black girl with freckles. She looked at him flashing a smile and he took that as the initiative to walk over to her and introduce himself. "I don't mean to stare, but you're beautiful. Can I have your name?" he asked, sounding like the kid he was. Khloe and Eazy sat across the room eyeing the two of them while cracking jokes.

"My name is Koi, and you are?"

"Ivory, how old are you?"

"Sixteen."

Ivory wanted to curse himself under his breath, he knew that once she found out his age that their conversation would be cut short. Although he could pass for eighteen, that wasn't what mattered. He wasn't willing to let her walk away without bagging her. This had been the first female to ever catch his attention, and he wanted her. He took a seat beside her and threw his arms around her shoulders. Wanting to withhold the truth from her, he decided against it. He knew it wouldn't be the best first impression.

"I turn fifteen next month, I'm throwing a party. You coming through with Khloe?" he asked, trying not to give his age too much attention. But Koi wasn't having it. She snapped her head and moved his arm from around her, looking at him.

"You a baby. What is you even doing up here? Khloe, what is this, a daycare?" Koi questioned, looking at her friend. Khloe began to laugh. She had known that once Koi found out Ivory's age, she would blow a gasket, and she was right.

"Koi, don't do him. My mans got his own crib, bread and fly as shit. Don't let that age shit fool you girl," Eazy stepped in defending his friend. Ivory put his hand up to stop Ezekiel. He was a man no matter his age and even though Eazy was his friend, he didn't need him speaking up for him.

"Listen Koi, you seem real bothered by a nigga's age. But that ain't stop a nigga from getting nothing he wanted in this world. I want you and I'mma have you whether you believe it or not. But you not gon' play me like some little nigga. So I'mma fall back and when you want you a real nigga, holla at me," Ivory stated while standing on his two feet and walking over to Eazy. He said his goodbyes before giving one last look at Koi. He had meant every word he said and knew that in time, she would be chasing after him and she didn't have to. But he wanted to show her who ran the show.

He walked out the house and jumped on his motorbike, reviving it up loudly while putting on his helmet. Just as he was about to pull off, he saw Koi out on the balcony staring at him. He had intrigued her, and he could tell all in her face. He gave a quick smirk before reviving up again and burning rubber down the street.

"Damn Khloe, that lil' nigga just might have me chasing his ass after all," Koi joked as she reentered the house. This time Ezekiel began to laugh. He knew that in no time Ivory would have her nose wide open.

"Oh so you finna run a daycare now?" Khloe joked. Koi rolled her eyes while picking up one of the couch pillows and tossing it at her best friend, laughing a lil' bit.

"Now I know I ain't have to say all that, but his age definitely took me by surprise," Koi explained.

Ezekiel rose up out his seat leaving Khloe and her friends in the living room, walking into the backroom going into the safe to count up his profit for the week. He neatly tied up the money with rubber bands and placed it in a Louis Vuitton backpack. Just as he was finished Koi was stepping into the office. "All the bread is there. Tell the boss I'm ready to move up too. Put the word in for a nigga K," Ezekiel told Koi, knowing that any word she put in would help him move up in ranks. Right now, he was running his own trap and touching major bread but he was greedy; he wanted to be the boss's number two. And because Koi was the boss's daughter, he thought getting in good with her would make him number two. But he was wrong, the boss would never make him or any of his other trap boys number two because that spot was safe and secured by Koi. Until she took over the drug game, there was no need for anyone else in command.

* * *

Ivory pulled up to Havoc's house and placed his helmet on his bike before knocking on the front door. When the door swung open Havoc let him in flashing him a smile. "What's good Ivory! Let me find out you done found yourself one of them young honeys and that's why you ain't been around." Ivory began to chuckle while shaking his head. He had enough time riding over to Havoc's house that he was able to place his feelings in check before getting here. And now he was putting on an Oscar worthy performance.

"Nah, ain't no honeys. Told someone my age today and they laughed." Ivory chuckled while thinking about Koi. He was smitten by her and they had barely spoken. In fact, she had practically dissed him, and he was still stuck up her ass.

Havoc began to laugh remembering those days as a kid that he had been turned down by girls because of his age, so much that it came to a point where he had begun lying about it. He lied until he didn't need to anymore. "Cyn and I put a plan together on how to get this nigga Biz, and I need you to be available to be on go. This time you coming with. Ain't no underestimating. It'll be next week. I'mma text you the details," Havoc explained to Ivory.

Just as he was about to respond, CJ walked in the room and when his eyes fell on Ivory they lit up like Hannukah candles. Ivory saw the look on CJ's face and instantly his mood had done a complete 360. "What's up lil' man?" he said walking over to CJ. CJ shrugged while giving him a high five. Ivory looked over at Havoc ready to ask if CJ was talking again, but Havoc's face said it all.

"How about we go to an arcade so I can beat you at some games," Ivory suggested. CJ nodded his head as a small smile came on his face. "Alright, go get dressed," Ivory instructed. He truly felt like a big brother. And he didn't mind it. He took a seat on the arm of Havoc's couch and they both sat in deep contemplation. Neither one of them saying a word to the other.

In five minutes, CJ was back downstairs, dressed in Spiderman from head to toe. Ivory gave him a smile while remembering the times where he was obsessed with Spiderman and would go out dressed identically to how CJ was dressed. "Aight Hav, I'll have him back in two hours," Ivory said while walking towards the garage to get his and CJ's bikes. He couldn't wait to get out of Havoc's presence. Every time he was around him at this point, he wanted revenge. He was tired of faking it; he hated him with everything in his body. He was glad that Havoc's mind was on this hit for Biz because now he wouldn't see it coming when Ivory planned out his hit on him.

CHAPTER 20

DATE NIGHT

"Baby you're no good, 'cause they warned me about your type girl. I been ducking left and right."

— THE WEEKEND

*B*onnie sat in the back of one of her favorite restaurants looking like she walked out of a magazine. Her strapless, red Donna Karan dress hugged her body like a glove. Since giving birth to the twins, her breasts and hips had gotten bigger and it gave her more body than she was used to. The cleavage she sported along with the high slit in her dress gave her more sex appeal than she was used to showcasing. She had turned heads with every step she took. Male and female, the attention was flattering. She looked at her watch on her arm impatiently. Biz was supposed to be taking her out for her birthday, but he was nowhere to be found. He had planned her entire day out and it went perfectly as planned but somewhere along the line, he dropped the ball. She had already been waiting on him for thirty minutes and she was over it. She put her finger up waving over to the waitress who had been gladly refilling her glass with wine all night and without a word, she was back with another glass.

"You gets a tip," Bonnie said, smirking as she downed the drink. Now Bonnie was no drinker, but she was almost sure she had drunk the entire bottle of wine at this point. In fact, she was almost sure the wine was the reason she hadn't stormed out already to find Biz and beat his ass. She chuckled at the thought while shaking her head. The night hadn't gone as planned, but just having a night out alone was enough and she would settle for that. She just hated that she had wasted an outfit. She had gotten all done up and didn't wear any panties because she just knew she was going to be throwing pussy at Biz. But nope, he was canceled for the night.

Just as she was about to get out her seat, she was taken aback by a man who stood just above her height and his skin was as dark as hers but his eyes were a hazel brown. "Now I know someone as fine as you ain't come here to be by yourself," he spoke in a deep baritone voice making her pussy cream. She didn't know if it had something to do with her drinking a whole wine bottle alone or if his looks alone were making her hot, but right now she was ready to bend over the table and let him blow her back out in front of all the patrons in the place. She stared at his lips and just wanted to feel them on her neck and most importantly on her southern lips. If she knew anything, she knew that this man could probably eat a mean pussy. On any other day of the week, she probably wouldn't even have given him any play. But it was her birthday and Biz had clearly stood her up.

"Bonnie, you are?" she asked, getting straight to the chase.

"Kannon, pleasure to meet you," he responded. Just as Bonnie was about to respond her voice got caught in her throat as Biz began walking up behind Kannon. Kannon could see the look on Bonnie's face without even turning around and knew it was his cue to leave. "I'll see you around Bonnie," he added while flashing her a smile of his pearly white teeth and walking away chuckling.

Bonnie just sat back down and looked at Biz. It was clear that he didn't like what he saw, but Bonnie shrugged. Had he been on time nobody would've had the audacity to step to her. "Nigga you need to fix your face. I been the one that's been sitting here for almost an hour waiting on ya late ass," Bonnie snapped.

Biz knew she was right and decided not to speak on what he had walked in on. He shook the way he was feeling off his shoulders and cleared his throat, now taking in her entire look. He reached over the table and put his hand through her short pixie haircut. "You cut it B?" he asked, surprised as he took a strand out her face.

"You like it?" she asked with a smile. She had been looking for a fresh new look and she had never tried a cut style. Biz nodded his head, loving the way it accentuated her face. "Thank you, but hell nah, I ain't cut my hair. This is a wig," she added while laughing.

Biz just shook his head while chuckling as well. "I'm sorry for being late B, but you know a nigga couldn't pull up empty-handed. My jeweler came by the house and this custom piece was made specifically for you." Biz apologized while pulling out a small box and passing it to her across the table. Bonnie tried not to show the excitement on her face, but it was of no use. Biz knew she loved jewelry so the only person she'd be faking for was herself.

As she opened the box her mouth dropped open as she stared at the diamond encrusted B necklace and earring set. She knew he'd paid a pretty penny for her gift the way it sparkled in the box alone, almost blinding her. The smile on her face was so wide that it made her cheeks hurt. "Oh, thank you, thank you, thank you, baby!" she exclaimed, not caring that she was a little loud. Biz chuckled at her as she danced in her seat like a kid. He knew she would love the gift. He didn't dare tell her that Missy helped him with the idea. He was happy that she was happy with it and that was all that mattered.

The two lovebirds sat across from one another indulging in conversation as if there was no one in the room except the two of them. They talked and laughed, like two kids on a first date and they knew it. Although they weren't kids, this had been their first real date and minus Biz's tardiness, Bonnie could say that she had really enjoyed herself. Biz had spared no expense on her for her birthday. It was her first birthday that she didn't celebrate with Havoc, and Biz had made it possible for that to not be a worry of hers. The sound of the waitress clearing her voice caused them both to look up at her. "I'm sorry, but we will be closing in fifteen minutes," she stated while passing them their checks and walking away. Bonnie looked around the restaurant, not believing that she and Biz were the last ones in there, and they weren't. Kannon was still inside, and he was staring Bonnie down with his eyes and undressing her. He licked his lips at her, and her pussy began to throb, and she couldn't believe it. She just began to hope that Biz didn't notice.

She cleared her throat while grabbing her clutch and standing up as Biz put the bills on the table. Her eyes reverted back to Kannon once more who was now chuckling. He knew exactly what he was doing to her and she didn't find it funny. She and Biz had just had an amazing date and she wanted it to continue. She knew that if Biz caught on everything would be a wrap. There would probably be bullets being rained down in the place and right now wasn't the time nor place. She was feeling cute, happy and just wanted some dick. She put her arm through his and followed as he led her out the restaurant.

Kannon stayed on her mind; she wanted to know who he was. He was super confident and didn't seem to care that there was a ring on her finger or the simple fact that she was on a date with her man. She knew whoever he was, he had to have some kind of power and authority over someone, or something. Because any ole average joe wasn't risking his life the way Kannon had. She shook him from her mind and decided she had thought enough about him; right now was about her and Biz. She wasn't wearing any panties and she was ready to fuck his brains out. The minute he stepped into the car she was all over him. He pulled back while starting the car. "We gon' handle that in the crib. Missy gotta get home," he spoke up.

All the lust that she was feeling instantly left her body. "What's up with her anyways? It's clear the bitch feeling you. How the hell you got her so open?" Bonnie asked suspiciously.

Biz laughed while looking at her, seeing that she was serious. "It ain't nothing ma, I promise. Look through my phone if you don't believe me. She just been helping out with the kids. That's it. Forget what you saw when you woke up. That's dead," he explained while passing Bonnie his phone. She grabbed it and thought about not going through it to show Biz that she trusted him, but the woman in her ate up the temptation and caused her to open up the phone.

She read the text messages between the two from the first day Missy had begun working at the house till current and nothing. Just as she was about to put the phone down, a silent text came through.

Unknown: It's Cyn, meet me at 3654 Lester Avenue. Tomorrow 8pm.

Bonnie's eyebrows raised at the text and all her red flags began popping up. She wanted to turn over and beat Biz in the head, but she didn't want to get too ahead of herself. She forwarded the text to her phone and deleted it from his. She was sure he wasn't messing with Missy, but this text had definitely piqued her interest. She replayed the name Cyn in her mind over and over to see if she remembered the name, but nothing came up. Instead, she played it cool. She didn't want anything to ruin her day for her. Plus, she needed some dick. Nothing, and she meant nothing, was going to get in the way of that. She put his phone down and he looked over at her. "You believe a nigga yet?" he asked.

Bonnie gave him a side smirk before replying, "Yea I believe you, but there is something you ain't telling me."

"She's Benny's wife," he stated, and Bonnie looked at him in surprise and it was as if the pieces of the puzzle began to put themselves together. She knew Havoc had killed Benny, and all the while she had been thinking that Biz had something going on with Missy when in reality, he had just been being a good Samaritan and helping out an old friend's family.

"Why didn't you just say that?" Bonnie asked while looking at him, feeling slightly guilty. He shrugged his shoulder and she just shook her head. She gave him a soft kiss on his lips and couldn't wait till they got home. She was ready to throw that thang down and put it on him.

As they pulled up in the driveway, Missy opened up the door on cue as if she had been impatiently waiting. As Bonnie and Biz exited the car and stepped to the front door, Bonnie took the initiative to speak up. "Thank you for watching them." Missy raised a brow in surprise but didn't say a word while directing her gaze to Biz while Bonnie entered the house.

"Did you drug her or something?" Missy joked. Biz chuckled, shaking his head.

"Goodnight Missy, we'll see you tomorrow," Biz replied before watching her get into her car and drive off.

CHAPTER 21

DEMANDS

"Thug nigga from the trenches never had a heart. Drug dealer, contract killer, loyal from the start."

— NBA YOUNGBOY

Missy laid in her bed rolling her eyes while Benny worked his tongue in between her legs. She had been celibate for the months that he was gone, and even though this moment should've had her in ecstasy, she wasn't. She had been turned off by him since he revealed that he was alive. And to be quite honest, she didn't believe a word he said about Biz. She hadn't said a word, instead just played along doing just as he said. She knew that if she tried anything different, she would feel Benny's wrath and she was sure that, that could almost end her life. The only thing that mattered was that Bee was happy. Because Benny was still laying low from Biz, Bee got to spend all the extra time that she had missed out on with him. Waking up and coming home from school to her daddy was like a dream she couldn't stop waking up from. Missy knew that Bee's happiness was most important but in the back of her mind she had wished that Benny really had died. She had already gone through the ropes of grieving, so him coming back was like a slap to the face.

"Ooh yess, Benny. Right there," Missy fake moaned. In fact, she wished that he would get away from her and stop touching her. Him leaving her and Bee still left a sour taste in her mouth. While he had left, Biz had helped her get back on her feet and he was the only person she wanted to caress her. She knew that would never happen, so she settled for Benny. It was crazy how another man could have you swoon just from the way he treated women and children. Have you wanting to forget the person of your past and wanting to pursue a future with them. That was how Biz had Missy and instead of shaking it off, she began to embrace it. It was the only way she could deal with Benny. She rubbed her hand on top of Benny's head and although he didn't have dreads like Biz, Missy just continued to tell herself it was Biz who was making her body feel good. The power of the mind worked in mysterious ways because Missy began grinding on his face while near an orgasm. "Right there Bi-enny," she said, managing to catch herself. She peeked out one eye to see if Benny had caught on to her almost name slip but he hadn't. He was so engaged and focused on her cumming. It was as if he had discovered the key to the treasure as he stuck one finger in her pussy and flicked his tongue on her clit. Almost instantly, Missy's body began to shake as she released an orgasm all over his face.

Benny sat up with a satisfied grin on his face. He pinned her legs up to her chest and began to rub his dick on the entrance of her pussy. He slid in slowly, embracing the feel of her warm walls. It was just as he remembered, and tighter. He knew she hadn't given up the cookie and that was all he cared about. Even though Missy couldn't stand the touch of Benny, his dick was undeniably big and fat, and he knew how to work it. She arched her back as her hands found a place on his back and began to scratch as she moaned loudly. As he pumped in and out of her, load moans escaped her lips. "Call me daddy," Benny instructed as he pulled out of her while she tried to push herself on top of him, but his grip on her didn't allow her to.

"Daddy, please fuck me." Her words were like magic to Benny's ears and also stroked his ego as he entered her going fast and hard, knowing that was just how she liked it. "I'm coming!" Missy screamed as he continued pumping because he was near his exploding point as well. In a matter of sixty seconds, he was shooting his seeds up in her and grinding slowly. He laid on his back once he emptied himself in her. Missy shot up from the bed and headed straight to the bathroom sitting over the toilet peeing, hoping that none of Benny's seeds managed to make it to her eggs. She already knew that with the way that she had been carrying on, if it continued, they didn't have a future with one another. She already had one kid by him that the two of them needed to focus on, she didn't need another. Nope, he wouldn't be disappearing on her again acting like he was dead leaving her with two kids. All those thoughts ran through her mind as she started up the shower.

She walked back into their bedroom and saw Benny lying on the bed as he went through her phone. It had become a habit of his since coming back. She knew that he was looking to see if he could find anything between Biz and her, but Missy was already two steps ahead of him. She made sure that everything that was sent through text was business only and that was how it remained. She ignored him, walking over to her dresser grabbing her small speaker and headed towards the bathroom. "You're quitting tomorrow."

Missy stopped in her tracks, looking at him as if he had grown two heads. "What?"

Benny looked up at her with a facial expression that said he was serious as a heart attack. "I'm home, everything is in place for that nigga to be a thought of the past. Now, you can live how we used to. You stay home with Bee and I get to the streets ma, what happened?"

"Benny, you left me for months! Thinking that you were dead. When that little bit of money you had saved up dried up, who had to go out and figure out how to do it as a single mother? Me! You cannot just come back and think you running shit again. I depended on you long enough, and you let me the fuck down," Missy responded, revealing all the pent-up aggression she had within her since Benny came back. It was the first time that she had raised her voice at him and from the look on his face, she could tell he didn't like it. He shot up from the bed and rushed over to her, getting so close that her back was against the wall.

"I said you quitting Missy, and I'm not gone say that shit again. I don't give a fuck about nothing you over here foaming at the mouth about. You heard what the fuck I said. Did I make myself clear?"

Missy didn't say a word, challenging him, and Benny couldn't understand who this was standing before him. He didn't see it as she had made a point, he saw it as she was rebelling against him for Biz, and that only further enraged him. He took his hand and wrapped it around her throat and squeezed as hard as he could. No amount of scratching at his hands made him loosen up this time. This was the last time he was allowing Missy to disrespect him. She hadn't done it in the past and he wasn't going to let her start now. He squeezed until Missy stopped putting up a fight then he finally stopped, letting her drop to the ground. She began to cough loudly while tears clouded her vision as she looked up at Benny in disbelief. "Did I make myself clear Missy?" Benny asked one more time.

Defeated, Missy nodded her head wildly, not able to speak because the knot in her throat wouldn't allow her to. She would quit her job, but that wasn't the only thing she would be quitting. She knew that if she didn't get away from Benny that he would slowly but surely kill her, and he wasn't worth it. He had left her before, and now she was going to make sure that she left him. She rose up off the floor as Benny went into the bathroom to clean himself up. As she saw him come back into the bedroom, she rushed by him going into the bathroom. She walked over to the mirror and tears began to form in her eyes again as the print of his hand was shown in bruise form around her neck. She stepped into the shower as her tears began to mix with the water that went down the drain. She couldn't believe that the man she had once loved, she despised. She wanted Benny to rot and die, but she didn't have the guts to do it herself. She knew the same way someone had attempted the first time they would attempt to again, and she couldn't wait until that day. But as for now, she had made up her mind that this was the last day that Benny would see her and Bee. She knew that Bee would have questions and that she would be putting her daughter through distress again, but she knew that the distance between them was what was best. Benny was showing her that he was capable of killing her, and she had someone to live for. Bee was her reason for everything, even the reason she ultimately had the strength to say she would be leaving Benny. She had to be a better example for her daughter. She couldn't stay and think she could give advice to her daughter if she was put in this same situation in the future.

She washed up her body and her hair. Feeling dirty, she just wanted to get the feel of Benny off of her. Once she felt cleansed, she rinsed off and got out the shower, wrapping a towel on her hair and one on her body. She looked in the mirror a second time, knowing that no amount of makeup could cover up that mark. Shame fell upon her as she entered the bedroom to a snoring Benny. He was laid out across the bed as if he was the man. But no, he was a coward and Missy wanted to grab a pillow and suffocate his ass in his sleep. But instead of doing that, she quietly tip toed around the room, thankful that Benny was a heavy sleeper as she grabbed her biggest suitcase and began throwing all the clothes of her and Bee's that she could fit inside.

After she stuffed up the suitcase, she threw on a pair of pajamas before lugging it out the house and into the garage, opening the trunk of her car and sticking the suitcase inside. She entered the house going straight into the kitchen and thinking of how exactly she would make her grand escape. She opened up the refrigerator grabbing the carton of Bee's orange juice and when she closed it, she was startled by Benny who was standing there staring at her. She didn't know what to think but she didn't say a word. She had nothing nice to say, and it was clear that everything that came out her mouth seemed to infuriate him. He walked over to her causing her to jump, and he shook his head as he slowly reached for her face. His hands roamed and touched the marks on her neck. Missy began to shudder, but Benny walked closer to her pulling her into a hug. "I'm sorry ma, a nigga ain't mean to. I'll never hurt you again," he said. Missy's eyes began to roll to the back of her head. This was that mind game shit that niggas liked to play with women to try and emotionally trap them, but Missy was over it and saw right through him. But she decided to play along because maybe him thinking she forgave him would make her grand exit easier.

"It's okay, I won't ever challenge you again," she said, which made her sick to her stomach. But it was music to Benny's ears; that was all he ever wanted. He kissed her forehead and grabbed her hand.

"Let's go to bed ma." Missy smirked behind him, quietly knowing that she had him exactly where she wanted him. In the blink of an eye, she would disappear from him and he didn't even know it.

CHAPTER 22

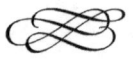

WOMAN TO WOMAN

"You shot your own brother; how can we know if we can trust Jay Z?"

— JAY-Z

Bonnie sat in the twins' nursery rocking Cassie in her arm while feeding her, singing along with Celine Dion. The kids had now begun to warm up to her, feeling their connection, and she couldn't be happier. She had realized that they just needed to spend more time with her and get to know her before they came to their senses, and they did. It took a little longer than she had expected but it happened. As she looked at the clock with every minute that went by, she thought about the text that Biz had received. She wanted to bring it to his attention but instead, she wanted to find out from the horse's mouth what was going on. A million thoughts ran through her mind and in every outcome, someone was gonna die. She had suspected Biz being with Missy and he had proven her to be wrong, but now this text from an unknown number piqued her interest. She was unsure if Biz really didn't communicate with anyone or if he really lived this life of a saint like he claimed to be. Biz was a good man and had proven to be time and time again, but that was what she had once thought about Khalil and that had turned out awfully. She knew in her heart that Biz was her soulmate and ultimately, she had given him 95% of her heart and the five percent remaining, she was unable to give. She didn't want to go through a heartbreak again. Biz had been one hundred with her and didn't give her any reason to think otherwise, but something about that text didn't sit right with her. she didn't know if it was because she had seen a woman's name in the text or if it was because the number was unsaved. Either way, she was in the dark about both and she had enough of secrets.

She looked down at Cassie, kissing her baby girl on the forehead seeing that she fell asleep. Bonnie had never experienced a feeling like this before towards any child. She had killed mothers along with their babies without a blink of an eye. She had never seen the significance when it came to children but now, here she was a mother that couldn't imagine what life would be like without her children. She rose out the rocking chair just as Biz was entering the room with a sleeping Cassidy. Bonnie just shook her head smiling at how in sync they were with their schedules. She laid Cassie down and gave her a kiss, then turned over to Cassidy's crib giving him the same love. They made her heart full to no extent. Biz wrapped his arms around her waist while kissing on her neck. His lips on her made her body quiver and if it wasn't thirty minutes until eight, she was sure that she would be taking him down. They had been having nonstop sex since she had been cleared and Bonnie was almost sure that her little hairstyle made Biz crave her even more. She couldn't deny it, she looked more mature and exotic with it. She was actually contemplating doing it with her real hair. But she was unsure because she could already see herself cursing herself out after it was done and over with. So for now, the short cut wig was gonna have to do.

"I love you B," he whispered in her ear.

"I love you too," she responded honestly. As his hands began to roam around her body, she took that as her cue to move. Right now she was on a mission and pleasing him would have to wait until she got back. "I'll be back, I need to run to the store to get some pads. My period will be here soon," she lied while spinning around and giving him a kiss on his neck. She walked out the room leaving his dick hard as a brick. He knew that the minute that she got back, he would be blowing her back out.

Bonnie walked out the room with her purse and phone in her hand. She had twenty minutes to get to the location, which was the perfect amount of time to her. She hopped in Biz's all-black, dark tinted Rolls Royce. She didn't want to be seen until she was ready to be seen, and this car did its job. She played her music while driving with her nerves slightly on edge. She didn't know what she was so nervous about. It was almost as if she was scared of the possibility of the truth being that Biz had been seeing someone else after she had given him so much of her. It would be a slap to the face, and she knew that if she and Biz didn't work, there would be no starting over or looking for someone new. That would make it enough for her to stop believing in love. Khalil and Biz had been the lucky ones to experience her love; anyone else after them didn't deserve to see that part of her. She was unsure if that part of her would still be around after the fact. She knew she wasn't going to be looking around to find out though. Her main priorities would be her children. She was set for life already; she had worked for the thrill of the kill. But Bonnie had saved up enough to live like a queen with her precious kids.

As she pulled up to the address, she realized it was a garage. It was empty and she drove to the very top where there was one other car in sight. She parked the car and waited for the woman in the other car to exit. Her eyebrows furrowed together as the woman that she had seen in the casino stepped out of the car. Just as she was about to step out, she noticed the passenger side door open as well and when the person came out, she realized that it was no one other than her twin brother. Panic began to set in once she realized that it was a set up. She reached for her phone and dialed Biz's number, tapping the steering wheel as she impatiently waited for him to answer. Just as she was about to hang up the phone, he answered. "Biz I—" Before she could get her full sentence out, her heart dropped into the pit of her stomach.

"Yes Biz, right there. Fuck me harder, I love you," she heard Missy moan. Her mind couldn't process what it was that she was hearing. She hung up the phone not wanting to hear any more, and it was as if Havoc's patience had run thin with who he thought was Biz. Just as Bonnie put the car in drive, bullets began to riddle the car.

Rat a tat tat, rat a tat tat

She ducked down in her seat screaming as she heard the automatic weapon continue to penetrate her car just as one hit her in the shoulder. It was obvious that Havoc had set this up. His hate for Biz ran so deep that he didn't care if they both had to lose their lives. As long as there was no breath left in Biz's lungs, Havoc would die a happy man. Bonnie grabbed the gun from under the driver's seat and began firing while still ducking. It was as if the machine gun had unlimited ammo because shots continued to ring out even when Bonnie's bullets were done. More bullets began to penetrate the car at the speed of lightning and Bonnie just knew that if she didn't get out of the car that she would be dead. But how could she when the bullets wouldn't stop. Rat a tat tat.

The bullets continued but this time, another one struck her in her side and on her thigh. With her adrenaline pumping, she knew her best bet was to remain where she was until the shooting stopped. She looked at the floor of the car seeing that she was losing a lot of her blood, and she began to get woozy. Panic began to set in, she had a reason to live and she couldn't go out like this. She tried relaxing her mind, filling her thoughts with images of Cassie and Cassidy. Reminding herself that they were her reasons to live. When the shooting stopped, the last thing she remembered hearing was Havoc walking over to the car and opening the door hoping to see a dead Biz. But once he saw that he had not in fact executed Biz, he began to curse under his breath. "SHIT! NO, WHAT THE FUCK B!" he said as he pulled his sister out the car. The death of many was on his hands and he could live with that, but the death of his sister, he couldn't. Although they fussed and fought every time they interacted, there was no way that he had wanted this for her. He had never lived a day without her. He had thought that he planned this all out precisely, not realizing that his sister would be caught in the crossfire. He had given Ivory, who was sitting on the roof of a building with a rifle, the okay to shoot the car up not thinking that it was Bonnie in the car. He had figured that Biz saw him and was getting cold feet. Once he had seen the car go back into drive, he knew he couldn't let Biz get away; it was now or never.

He felt her pulse and stared up at Cyn who was at a loss for words. Havoc hadn't told her that he was gonna light the car up so this was all a shock to her. She had planned on talking to Biz and the minute the bullets rang out, in the pit of her stomach sorrow filled her. But seeing that it wasn't Biz in the car somewhat eased her nerves, but she was still baffled. She had no idea where the other bullets had come from, but she knew Havoc had planned this part behind her back. "What did you do!" she screamed at him with tears in her eyes. She had only known Havoc for a few months, and she was finally seeing him as the monster he was. She had ignored the fact that he had killed Vee in cold blood, but this right here, she couldn't ignore. Tears began to fall from her eyes as she watched Havoc with the same shocked expression he had. She could tell that Havoc regretted it now, but it was too late.

He sat on the floor doing chest compressions on Bonnie hoping that she would hold on. He wasn't giving up on her without a fight. He couldn't give up on his sister. No matter how hard they fell out. "Come on B, don't give up," he stated while pushing on her chest.

He looked at Cyn who was just standing there and like a switch, he was pissed. "Call the fucking ambulance!" he yelled, causing Cyn to jump. She pulled her phone out her pocket and he listened as she gave them the address. "They on they way B, come on sis. You gotta live for my niece and nephew," he tried encouraging her, hoping that she could hear him. Once Cyn got off the phone the sound of a hammer being pulled back on a gun could be heard. Havoc continued the chest compressions not caring that the barrel of a gun was pointed behind his head. Right now, the only thing that mattered to him was the survival of his sister. As the person with the gun came from behind him and stood face to face, Havoc was shocked to see that it was Ivory. He knew exactly what this was about and didn't try to reason with him. He had made a beast out of Ivory and now that beast had come back to haunt him.

"Ivory, I'm sorry," Havoc apologized while still pressing on Bonnie. The sirens could be heard, and he just needed to continue for a little longer till the ambulance got there.

"Ain't no sorry nigga. I could've shot you behind your back like you did my mother and father, but I'm not a coward like you," he spat while his emotions began to take over him. Havoc could see the unsureness in Ivory, but he didn't try to talk him out of it. Bonnie's blood was on his hands and it wasn't something he could live with.

"Shoot me!" Havoc yelled causing Ivory to jump. Cyn stood in the background not knowing what to do. This was all too much for her. This wasn't her lifestyle. She watched as Ivory and Havoc went back and forth, just hoping that she wasn't next. "B, I'm sorry," Havoc said one last time while closing his eyes waiting to receive his fate.

CHAPTER 23

BIG MISTAKE

"I think I started something, I got what I wanted, can't feel nothing, superhuman."

— FRANK OCEAN

The minute Bonnie walked out the front door Biz entered the kitchen grabbing the bottle of the wine he and Missy had once drank before. He grabbed a glass and began to pour. "Can I join you?" Missy asked as she entered the kitchen. He shrugged his shoulders and she grabbed a glass filling it for herself while standing in front of him. She had been contemplating telling him all day that she had to quit, but she didn't know how. And now that the night had come to an end, she couldn't prolong it. "Today is my last day with the twins," she built up the courage to say. Biz raised a brow while looking at her confused.

"Did B say something to you?" he asked, and Missy shook her head from side to side.

"No, actually, she's been too damn nice," she tried to joke, but Biz was still looking for an answer on why she was quitting. "Benny is back," she added, looking at Biz to see if that news made his demeanor change, but it didn't. Instead, he nodded his head in understanding. It was news to him but news that he didn't care for. If Benny was back, that meant that he would be going after Havoc making Biz's job easier for himself, he thought.

"Well it was nice having you as a nanny, the kids love you," Biz complimented as he looked at Missy. He could see that something else was troubling her and although he wanted to just ignore it, he couldn't. "Wassup ma?" he asked as he pulled her in closer to him knowing that, that would make her more comfortable. It made her comfortable but the feeling of his hands on her waist made her pussy thump. She swallowed the lump in her throat while looking up at him. She placed his hand on her chest making him feel her heartbeat as she placed her hand on his. Just as she had thought, both their hearts were racing at the same speed.

"You feel that?" she questioned.

Biz nodded his head knowing exactly what she was talking about, but he removed his hand. "I only feel this with you, not with Benny. Not with anyone else but you," she whispered.

He put his hand on her face making her look directly into his eyes. "You ain't mine ma, Bonnie is for me and Benny is for you," he tried to explain, hoping that she would agree, but she didn't.

"Benny isn't for me," she replied, offended. She knew that Biz had no idea where her aggression was coming from and decided to show him instead of talking. She calmly pulled off the scarf that she had been wearing all day. Biz had thought maybe it was because it was a part of her outfit, so he didn't question it but as she slowly took it off, he realized that she was covering up a bruised neck. Instantly a flame lit up in him. "Who did this Missy?" he asked while his nose began to flare. His reaction to it made Missy have butterflies, but her response was what made tears fill her eyes.

"Benny," she said in a little over a whisper. Biz looked at her puzzled and a million questions rummaged through his mind. He placed his hand over the bruise and shook his head. He couldn't understand why Benny would want to put his hand on a woman so beautiful. Missy was like a delicate flower; Biz couldn't see her doing or saying anything out of the ordinary to deserve this.

"Where that nigga at?" Biz questioned. He didn't put himself in other people's drama, but he had felt a sense of security when it came to Missy, like she was now his responsibility.

"Home with Bee," she responded. Biz nodded his head taking note.

"You don't gotta go tonight if you don't want to. We got spare bedrooms. Don't worry about B, I can talk to her. But don't be out here endangering yourself when you don't have to," he explained, but Missy shook her head.

"I gotta get Bee," she replied in a panicked tone. Although Benny had never hurt their daughter, she didn't put anything past him. There had been a time when he had never raised his voice or a finger to her, and now look where she was standing. It was clear that he'd changed, and she couldn't leave her baby girl with him.

"Don't worry about Bee, I'll go get her first thing in the morning. You do enough for my kids, so I can help you out with yours. Just give me her school schedule and I'll be there and if she stays home with him, I'll go up in there and get her," he offered.

Missy looked up at him to see if he was serious and the look on his face confirmed it. She didn't know how to thank him and in fact, there were not enough words to express how thankful she was for him. He was trying to deny what he felt for her but Missy knew she wasn't crazy. If he didn't feel anything for her, he wouldn't have been willing to go out his way for her like he was about to do. His words gave her confirmation that he did care about her and more than you would care about your average nanny. It gave her the courage to do what she had been wanting to do for the longest. She put her lips together bringing them up to him while wrapping her arms around his neck. She didn't care that he wasn't hers right now. But here in this moment, she wanted to feel him. She thought he would pull away from her and was surprised when he didn't. He ran his hand through her hair and returned the kiss. Their tongues began to get intertwined with one another as they swapped DNA. Biz knew everything about this was wrong but decided to go along anyways. He had been avoiding Missy for long enough and it was clear that they both had already crossed the line. His hands ran down her back and stayed on her ass. He squeezed it causing a light moan to escape her lips. Bonnie had left him with a hard-on already and now Missy was about to help him with it. He picked her up in his arms as she wrapped her legs around his waist, and he walked out the kitchen while holding her under her ass and all the way to his bedroom. All of his common sense had seemed to go out the window. It was as if Biz had left the building and his alter ego Pleasure had walked in, because the one thing Biz knew how to do best was not mix business with pleasure. But here he was about to give Missy the best dick of her life. But not before he pleased her the best way he knew how. He laid Missy onto the bed and pulled her pencil skirt up and her panties down. He admired her love box for a second then stuck two fingers inside which made her moan out loud. As he fingered her, seeing how wet she became made his dick turn brick hard, but he was a gentleman at all times even when it came to sex; he wanted to please the ladies first. He used his tongue to part her southern lips and began to suck, slurp and lick up every drop she released. As his fingers penetrated her pussy, he used another finger to penetrate her ass all at the same time. "Oh, shit Biz I'm fucking cumming!!" Missy screamed as he worked on her like a piece of art. He pulled back from her and looked at her with lusty eyes.

"Get on your hands and knees," he instructed, and she did just that. She couldn't wait to feel him in her. The length of his dick and the girth of it told her she would be running in no time. But with the way that he used his tongue, she knew he had to know how to use his piece. As she got on all fours, a smile crept on her face. Just yesterday she had been imagining he was pleasing her and now here he was putting it down on her so good, she was almost sure she wouldn't be able to walk afterwards. He entered her pussy from behind and began pumping in and out of her with speed. Just like she thought, she began running from the dick that he was putting on her. Benny didn't have nothing on him. He was so indulged in blowing Missy's back out that he didn't realize that his phone was silently ringing on the nightstand. Missy moaned loudly as she realized the phone through her peripheral vision and sneakily reached over, answering it.

"Yes Biz, right there. Fuck me harder, I love you," Missy made sure to moan loud enough to be heard through the phone. If Biz wouldn't leave Bonnie, she was sure that as a woman hearing this, Bonnie would leave Biz which would give her all access to him and this dick. It was crazy how he had her acting out in ways that she never had. It wasn't like she was dickmatized, because this was the first time she got the dick. She didn't know any other way to express it except that she was in love with Biz and would do almost anything to have him. If it meant fucking up a happy home, so be it. His kids loved her anyways and the way he was with his kids, she knew that he would be like that with hers. The thought of them being together made her explode all over his dick. He was working it just like she knew he could. He had shown her what he could do and now it was time for her to return the favor. She pulled away from him, letting his dick slide out, and laid him on the bed. She climbed on top of him while slowly easing down on him until she was all the way down. She ran her tongue across his chest making sure to lick both of his nipples before she planted her feet flat on the bed and began bouncing on him, like she had a trampoline beneath her. Biz squeezed his eyes shut as the feeling of her ass bouncing on him made his dick want to shoot cum in her. He grabbed her waist trying to slow her down, knowing that if she didn't then she would possibly be baby mama number two, but Missy wasn't having it. She had allowed him to have his fun, now it was her turn.

The two were so engaged in their sexcapade that neither one of them could feel the presence of another person in the room. "BANG!" a gunshot rang out and instantly Missy's head went crashing down onto

Biz's chest. He could feel the blood leaking out of her head onto his chest but knew he had no time to think right now; he had to act. With the speed of a cat, Biz reached over to his nightstand grabbing his loaded 9mm letting off a shot, hitting the person who had invaded his home straight in the forehead. He heard the body drop but decided to use that to his advantage to get up and unload his entire clip in the person. With every shot he took, he took another step forward making sure to overkill. His blood was racing and so was his mind. When he got close to the person, he shook his head when he saw that it was none other than Benny. He didn't feel any sympathy for him; in fact, he felt like he deserved every bullet that he placed in him. Biz shook his head from side to side knowing that Benny must have followed Missy to his home. But what he didn't understand was why Benny would come after him guns blazing. But the dead couldn't speak, and Biz knew that all his questions would remain unanswered. He shook his head knowing that he had fucked up. Here he was in his house butt ass naked with two dead bodies on his bedroom floor. Instantly, he grabbed his shorts that he had been wearing off the floor and rushed out the room while grabbing Benny's gun as well. He rushed to the nursery to make sure the twins were straight, and his mind was somewhat at ease knowing that they were fine. He began to search the entire house plus its perimeter to make sure that Benny was alone. Once he was done, Biz just shook his head from side to side, then Bonnie came to mind. He rushed up to the bedroom grabbing his phone off the nightstand seeing that she had called him, and it had been answered. Nothing but the worst thoughts began to rummage through his mind. Had Benny gotten to her? As he called her phone, he waited for an answer but instead got the voicemail. He didn't know what to think and in the pit of his stomach, he didn't think of nothing but the worst. He knew something was wrong. When his phone began to ring and Bonnie's name came across the screen, he began to feel of a little more comfort.

"B, you good?" he asked as soon as he answered.

"Biz, it's Cyn, there was a shootout."

"Thank you for Reading Devoted to an Outlaw, I hope you all enjoyed. This isn't the end. Stay on the look out for my spin off that will answer all your questions.
Details will stay posted on my Facebook Page:
Authoress Dak"

ABOUT THE AUTHOR

My name is Diaka Kaba and I am from the Bronx, NY. I have always had a passion for reading since the third grade. At the time Barbara Parks Junie B. Jones series were godly to me. As I got older picking up The Coldest Winter Ever by Sister Soulja is what got me hooked to Urban fiction. I began writing on Wattpad for fun and I got signed to my first publishing company Shan Presents. When I became a teen mom I put the pen down for a while then realized that every job I worked made me miserable and that writing was my true passion and what made me happy. The author who inspires me the most is Ashley Antoinette. My dream is to one day become New York's Best Selling Author.

Stay Connected:
Email me questions at DIAKASKABA@GMAIL.COM
I will be answering questions about Honesty and Ahmad on my YouTube channel, DAK's Corner.

Royalty Publishing House is now accepting manuscripts from aspiring or experienced urban romance authors!

WHAT MAY PLACE YOU ABOVE THE REST:

Heroes who are the ultimate book bae: strong-willed, maybe a little rough around the edges but willing to risk it all for the woman he loves.

Heroines who are the ultimate match: the girl next door type, not perfect - has her faults but is still a decent person. One who is willing to risk it all for the man she loves.

The rest is up to you! Just be creative, think out of the box, keep it sexy and intriguing!

If you'd like to join the Royal family, send us the first 15K words (60 pages) of your completed manuscript to submissions@royaltypublishinghouse.com

LIKE OUR PAGE!

Be sure to LIKE our Royalty Publishing House page on Facebook!

LEOPARDI

CPSIA information can be obtained
at www.ICGtesting.com
Printed in the USA
LVHW091715120619
621002LV00005B/781/P